To dear
With w
shared many
wondrous "journeys"...

With love,

Mom

Then Let the Barrier Fall

Also by Nomi Sharron

non-fiction

Tony Samara:
A Modern Shaman... and Beyond

plays

On the Road to Jerusalem

Black Box
based on the novel by Amos Oz

Then Let the Barrier Fall

by

Nomi Sharron

New Generation Publishing

Published by New Generation Publishing in 2015

Copyright © Nomi Sharron 2015

First Edition

The author asserts the moral right under the Copyright, Designs and Patents Act 1988 to be identified as the author of this work.

All Rights reserved. No part of this publication may be reproduced, stored in a retrieval system or transmitted, in any form or by any means without the prior written consent of the author, nor be otherwise circulated in any form of binding or cover other than that in which it is published and without a similar condition being imposed on the subsequent purchaser.

www.newgeneration-publishing.com

for anthony

and for kharis

"I give you half of me;
No more lest I should make
A ground for perjury.
For your sake, for my sake,
Half will you take?

"Half I'll not take nor give,
For he who gives, gives all.
By halves you cannot live;
Then let the barrier fall,
In one circle have all."

>from Circle and Square,
>in Edwin Muir's "Collection"

In the Beginning was the Word...

One

I turn into St. Margaret's Street and stop on the corner, grappling to contain the fear inside my anticipation; to greet old sights with new eyes. But which face of history will Canterbury disgorge: legend or celebration or a pilgrim's dark tale? They say that pilgrims' secrets, lying unburied, whisper down the centuries, snaring newcomers and terrifying the old. But my pilgrimage to Canterbury is of another kind. My tale is not bawdy; it hardly offers juicy titbits to the prurient. Yet it still manages to draw darts of disapproval from the pious and the prim.

Slowly, the city unwrinkles itself in spasms of red brick and pink flesh. But it smiles no recognition of secrets we once shared. The cobblestones are dusted with footsteps paving new stories; walls yield no imprint of a lover's kiss. Smoky city sounds swallow his voice; Richard's voice. Sounds breathing betrayal. For a city is a whole world when you love someone in it.

Dressed in borrowed nonchalance, I mingle with the throng of family shoppers: mothers with scolding faces, fathers with absentee eyes, mulish children out of school and into mischief. I stare into furniture shops, bustling with young couples buying three-piece-suites on the never-never, and wonder what the market price of happiness is today. Further up, I pass the bookshop where we used to browse and exchange furtive looks among the second-hand books.

Familiar sights allow me to pretend that I belong. The old beggar sits moaning softly in his appointed place outside the bespoke tailors, rolling his blind eyes heavenwards in stunted longing. He is still wearing his long matted hair and sulky beard, and looks more than ever like a grumpy biblical prophet of doom. Next to his tattered hat his dog, with mournful eyes, begs in his place.

I throw some coins into the hat and walk on quickly, embarrassed by his need, or mine. The street narrows and buildings moan, heavy with the weight of history. The power of stones to hold human experience is palpable. Weaving familiar patterns, the cobbles trip up my memory.

Richard... your face jumps out at me around every corner: that marvellous face, glowing like light in a Vermeer painting breaking free from the paint. But as I reach out to touch you, strangers stare incomprehension through naughty eyes. And that condescending bitch, Today's Reality, vomits up a plethora of new facts to drown old truths. Sighs, buried in the bowels of the earth, wait for volcanic release.

Dry dust of late summer grazes my sandalled feet. Forgotten scenes, caught in a flash by the camera of time and continuously replayed. Remembered scenes... And places I don't recognize; the city changing more quickly than the human heart.

The spirit of place, the old longing, wraps me in a kind of homesickness for unfinished biographies. I ache to discover the real journey of those days that gave all for love. Drawn back by a tug of the heart; or by whimsy – a will o' the wisp, whispering seductively in the dark. Or perhaps by a need to recover, to record; to unbind the syntax of memory...

Richard standing by the stage door, silent, watching, waiting... The seductive glow of his pipe beckoning to me in the dark. His eyes unpacking time. And we recognizing, in the way we unfold the moment, that we have awakened in each other's dreams.

I sit on a little bench in Rose Square, watching Canterbury coil around the lives of its inhabitants: ingesting the unreliable human condition, eructing waves of despair, loneliness, belief. Weaving its own stories: profound, provocative or prosaic. Shuddering up dreams from its fabled foundations. I stare as it jumbles the debris of old dramas we thought our own, but perhaps were really the city's, writing its memoirs with our lives. Though it is we who carry its scars in our hearts.

It starts to rain lightly, washing the carpet of dust on the cobbles into abstract paintings. I take shelter in the oak-beamed tearoom, cosy with gossiping gentility. This is where we sat and said meaningful things to each other over tea and scones. Small moments, snatched from obscurity by a trick of the light.

Outside, the streets are littered with the whitening bones of past passions; scraps of misjudged improvizations of the heart. How shall I begin to decipher the writing on the wall? Guilt-paved alleys offer no clues. Ancient bricks bleed only forgetfulness to mist the scaffolding of faith. I stumble on the loose stones of the past, buried, but not dead.

The city dissolves and recomposes itself in the late afternoon haze, tempting me with old secrets and new possibilities. But I no longer recognize it, nor those carving new pilgrimages across its flagstones. Apathy droops on strangers' faces, sorrow scratches at places where love once reigned. Memory, catching sight of itself in the glass window, recreates its own innocent painting of the past...

****

Night: dark sky slashed with orange stars, more beautiful over Canterbury than elsewhere.

A thin Muslim moon waits virgin-shy for a lover's first caress. Expectancy hangs like ripe apples on the trees, dispelling the last core of doubt.

Holding hands, we shuffle along narrow streets towards future implications. ["Tread softly, for you are treading on my dreams..."] How innocent I was!

The pubs dispel their last dribble of drinkers, onto pavements cracked with dried-out hope. Raucous laughter and the sweet dry smell of beer spill into the night. But we are already intoxicated.

Lighted windows beckon down the street, beacons of belonging; people in identical little boxes living and loving and dying slowly. Rooms seen from the outside, hiding paradoxes behind neat net curtains. How willingly I would abdicate the world, just to belong in a small anonymous room with Richard. But the world refuses to go away.

'What despairing details forge the chains of others' reality,' I say, trying to impress him; to deflect my longing.

'Chaos exists only in the human mind; technological attrition of the soul! The more facts we appropriate, the less we really know.'

'Well, we all make our own arrangements with the devil!'

'Yes? And what are yours?'

'That he will give me what God withholds.' The words tumble out of my mouth before I know what I've said. But sound ominously prophetic.

I can't see but feel your smile brush the back of my neck with promise.

'Aren't you a little young to have given up searching in God's domain?' he teases.

Well, my searching anywhere is over. I have found the one. THE one. Though I didn't know I was seeking. The one who makes my blood cascade and the world spin; the pulse vibrating in the miracle darkness, the unnameable mystery of my dreams made flesh. Explosion and stillness. Love, touching the edges of the divine.

Dear God, let finders be keepers, just this once. I'll never ask anything more of you. Ever. I'll even try to pray if you like.

But there would be time for prayer hereafter. Now, the miracle hangs across the sky, ripe with hope; and the Pillar of Fire guides our steps and our confirmation.

At the door of my digs, Richard takes my hand, and I am smothered over by this moment's measureless purity. When time begins to move again, we smile our felicitations for the night.

* * * * * * *

Halfway down St. Margaret's Street the theatre squats, burdened with old memories it didn't choose. Strung out on a meridian between panic and expectation, I approach The Marlowe, redolent of greasepaint and props and make-believe; though the real drama of those days was played out off stage.

I go round the back and cross the car park to the stage door. I stare at it, willing it to divulge some secret sign of recognition. But it stares back with wounding unconcern. And suddenly I am afraid: of what I might see; of what I might not see.

A very young, dark-haired actress emerges, so naive, so vulnerable, so impatient to carve her life across her unprotected soul. I reach out to her, overwhelmed with tenderness, but I cannot rewrite her biography. The selective fictions that we weave with our lives may be written in invisible ink, but leave permanent stains on our consciences. Behind her, in the shadows, stands a man with unreadable eyes, smoking a pipe, watching, waiting...

But the image of my younger self dissolves as I pass the theatre, walking blindly into the clutches of history. I try to pin down the pavement with moments of past grace. But the colours spill over the edge of my power to retain them; paint another's picture. Signposts disintegrate as I approach, and all meaning dissolves in the haphazard embellishment of newer facts. How shall I decipher the codes glinting at the end of the road? How shall I reach discernment?

But at the end of the road, it's the vast magnificence of the Cathedral that juts out to greet me, not ciphers dissembling disaster. It, too, is dressed in borrowed habits, and winks no collusive eye. Once, it hung promiscuous shadows across our nights bursting the seams of desire. Later, the spire gored us, and drew blood. But the gods were not placated.

I look up, but not with thoughts of prayer. Death again seduces me, the ultimate consummation. I think of cliff-tops, and the wild Welsh sea raging below, waiting to dash my reflection to perpetuity on the rocks. And Richard, winding a bridal shroud of seaweed through my hair...

But my shadow, weighted with future hours, smiles up at me, enticing me with hope. No, my celestial tormentors, my last embrace will not be round this huge holy phallus. The joke's too sick.

Dusk descends without warning, and the cooling air cuts across all reverie. I remember that I've forgotten to eat.

* * * * * * *

At the "Inn of Happiness", on one of those early evenings between knowing and knowing, gaudy Chinese mirrors reinvent our guarded looks of longing. Waiters with small hands and obsequious smiles serve us spare ribs and egg fried rice. It is the first time I have ever eaten pork; a sin of such gravity that I wait in mounting fear for the ground to open up and swallow me.

My childhood bulged with the laws of Orthodox Judaism: six hundred and thirteen commandments to keep me pure and observant. Though to be 'observant' did not mean to see. We were separated from our neighbours by a small garden fence, and centuries of Jewish Tradition. I imbibed with my mother's milk the collective consciousness of my race: bloody wars, brutal conquests, pitiless persecution; heroes flayed alive for refusing to bow to a human emperor, or swallow a morsel of pork. History, with an agenda.

The ancestors scrape about inside my skull, demanding acknowledgement. Old women's eyes weeping warnings that lance my heart. Old men with long beards and short smiles spy on my naked defiance. There is a price, you know. And the smell of my childhood, binding me, binding me...

Betrayal is ugly, but it is swift. I eat pork. I renounce all even symbolic separation from Richard. Defiantly peeling off garments that had kept me snug but too safe, I forgo my dubious status as one of God's Chosen People, and leap into the world without a safety net to catch me as I fall. And I fall! But the ground doesn't open up and devour me. Though I know that my perdition is already decreed. But not for this. You named my sin, my ministering angels, then broke the bargain. And my pain, though huge, was not enough to assuage my guilt.

Mesmerized by your eyes, I steal sidelong glances behind my well-bred smoke-screen. I eat with chopsticks and little expertise. And you watch me, and watch me, the smile of the Sphinx creasing your face with curiosity. The shape of beginnings.

Playfully, we pull a Chinese cracker, and Confucius jumps out: "Many seek happiness higher than man, others beneath him; but happiness is the same height as man."

'But first one must know the height of man. And the quest can take a lifetime,' you say, with mock gravity.

Mine is over, I thought. He is not very tall, and smokes a pipe, and has long sensual fingers, and talks to me of John Donne. And his eyes hold my world captive.

I talk too much, abusing words to mask my nervousness. Later, you tell me you were flattered that I should try so hard to impress you. Oh, the rueful artifices of love!

I try to lock my lips, but I cannot stop the questions that are falling out of my mouth.

'What do you write?' I ask, struggling to sound impersonal as a grave-digger.

'Words, words, words.'

'And do you also feign madness to survive an insane world?'

'Well, my dear, you shall be my judge.'

Judge, no. Maybe your Counsel for the Defence. 'But seriously, what do you write?'

'Seriously? I write poetry. Very seriously. "... out of key with his time, he strove to resuscitate the dead art of poetry to maintain the 'sublime' in the old sense." Ezra Pound.' His smile assumes my knowledge; wrongly.

'Of course.'

You look at me, burning holes in my friable defences. My wax wings are already melting.

I search for words that will not betray my ardour.

'And – what brings you to Canterbury?'

'Well, my little inquisitor, there is work to be done here.' He is silent; then catches my look of too unguarded innocence, and relents. 'I'm working on a group of what I suppose could be called poems of the sacred, which I hope to stage – no, that's not the right word, to *celebrate* – at the Cathedral. Croft has agreed to "lend me" some of the actors from the Marlowe.' Then, as if an afterthought, 'Perhaps we shall work together?'

I muster a lame smile. Speech has jilted me.

'I'm fascinated by the whole *process* of theatre; words jumping off the page into people's mouths, growing a life of their own. And then,' – with a smile to defeat all resolution – 'I have a weakness for beautiful young actresses.'

But how did you know I would be here, I think. What I say is, 'I'm not beautiful.' Defined as pretty from birth, I had not suffered easily the implied limitations of this description. It was Richard who granted the synthesis, who gave me back my face replete.

'Who mentioned you?' he teases. And his eyes tease; in another way.

* * * * * * *

In a small room above The Pig and Whistle pub behind the theatre, I sit and reflect. A gnarled creaky bed, a chipped wash-bowl and water jug and a faded armchair, claim their dusty space – nothing either to please the eye or distract the mind. My shadow nudges me. She is bent towards me in a gesture of solicitude, seducing me with courage. She hovers, tantalizing, over the keys of my typewriter, waiting...

But what is my task? To pin down the symbols of memory on paper, to distil the raw materials of my life, to uncoil its form? Writing in order to save myself? To set myself free? Coming back to this city where love first found us, coming back to try to uncover the truth of those days... But is it ever possible to deconstruct the nature of truth? For the person remembering is not the same person who experienced those events, exactly because living through them has changed me. And surely it is this very fact that distorts their memory? But it is also this journey, between the lines of the experience and its memory, that provides such potent raw material for the writer in me to decipher. And maybe one day, if the universe smiles on me, I shall reach that illusive goal of the writer – of any artist – Meaning. At the very least, perhaps I shall finally be able to allow myself some compassion.

What remains to be done then but to pick over the bones left by the psychoanalysts? For the real mystery of truth lies beyond the scope of mind scavengers; it is reached by an act of divination, as it were, from the guts, the entrails of emotion manifest in action. And no-one is born just once.

I poke about in the dustbins of experience, to see what may be salvaged from the wreckage. But whose truth shall I uncover in the debris? For each moment remembered is two moments, his and mine. Or three moments, history's, his and mine. Or many moments, colliding briefly, exploding on impact. Raining fallout to pen a new mythology.

Truth, trickling through the trough of memory.

Richard... The first time I saw you: standing at the door of the rehearsal room, a Greek god bearing unknowable gifts. Your chiselled face full of untold stories; promise of danger, and a warm hearth in winter. Fleetingly, your eyes find mine; stay to reconnoitre. Smile. And in that smile, the heartbeat of the world, bestowing grace.

I curl along roads that wind like arterial wounds, searching for tools to excavate the past; not as chronology, the resin of history; but rather to allow the past to reveal itself in the sequence of its significance. To uncover the bones of meaning; the language of the soul. But there is only one significant fact, and that lies buried too deep to be mined.

The insolence of the city crawls under my skin. The old market place stained with echoes of our future wounds, as well as England's bloody past. But Canterbury, I love you, for in the cabalistic shadows of your Cathedral I first loved Richard. And how can we help but love a place that has made us suffer deeply?

Now, cracking open memory, I see that it can recreate only a gesture, a look, a word spoken in haste, or unspoken; but the mystery at the heart of our fractured interlocking lives remains illusive. Only the pain remains.

I follow my feet to where the crowded streets fall into a rough open space, and trees provide a refuge from the stares of an inquisitive world. But I am not safe; a small boy is kicking pebbles across my illusions of solitude, and my foot slips clumsily over the grave of my mind's eye...

* * * * * * *

When I first came here, the world was smiling with lazy good will. The first breath of March whipped up the dust to write a renaissance across the cobbles.

Puffed-up almond blossoms, newly fallen, grazed the ground with rose-tinted promise. The berries were ripe on the trees.

When I first came here I was innocent, and still believed that air disasters and infidelity only happen to other people. I had come to read a new play. I had come to think about a man who had fallen into my dreams, leaving in his wake a whirlpool of exquisite confusion.

And what did I know of this man who gatecrashed my life with such ease? Nothing; except that he has tousled mousy hair, and writes poetry, and his eyes make waterfalls of my blood. Everything.

As excuse to myself for such monstrous self-indulgence, I dip into the play: "Lovers... I have imagined what they do and what they say – these lovers. It seems they find great delight in music and solitude, in touching and nakedness, in night."

Will everything I ever read now bring me back to Richard? My heart unravels with longing; words queuing up to be spoken, dissolve in the disrespectful air. Moments becoming memories, before they are lived.

"And from these things they make a fabric of memory which will serve them well in their life after death, when they will be together but alone. They are wise, for that is the purpose of any memory – of any experience – to give foundation to the state of death... The words were spoken during our lifetime, it is the memory which causes the unrest."

Yes. I didn't know, then...

And next week Hillary, and not I, will be given the part of Stella.

I walk away, not careful enough to avoid the riot of nettles proving that the idyll is not perfect. To someone who sees the capricious hand of Fate in too many places, I should have recognized this ill augury of the future. But today the sun is shining. I shall leave tomorrow's fears for tomorrow.

* * * * * * *

At the first rehearsal of Boris Vian's "The Empire Builders" [how portentous!] we sit in a ragged circle, a few smoking, musing or attentive, some bright, some concerned, some neither, bound in our need to wear other people's lives, perhaps to escape our own.

Croft reads from the stage directions: "'... a room with no special character, furnished in a conventional manner... windows with closed shutters, doors leading wherever necessary...'"

A stranger is standing at the door. He is not handsome, he is not tall, he has tousled mousy hair. Why has the world gasped and held its breath? The Ides of March is still a week away! Or is it only I, projecting unarticulated desires onto a stranger whom my soul has always known? Reality turned out-side in. Shadow play, or a Chinese lantern theatre. Plato's cave.

Croft cuts rudely across my imaginings: 'Danielle, read the notes on Zenobia.'

"'I had my own room painted blue like for a boy... through the window I could see the green trees... they were years with twelve months of May, months of May with thirty-one Sundays...'"

And then you look at me, your brow creased into a question-mark, a hint of laughter playing havoc with your lips. And your eyes hold mine, the shared instant stretched between us, and smile affirmation.

And suddenly I am overwhelmed by sadness, that no-one has ever recognized me before.

* * * * * * *

History as truth. Truth as memory. Memory recorded as history. Or, memory as truth. Truth as history. History recorded as memory. Infinite revolutions, encoded in the ethos, spiralling outwards to eternity. The shadow of the world interrupted on its journey, caught unawares, recaptured. The invisible orbits of the stories we were writing with each other's lives.

Memory: the judgement of history. Memory: the scar tissue of love.

* * * * * * *

Midnight, the witching hour. As I approach my digs, bedraggled and out of breath, a tiny glow beckons me through the syrupy blackness: the disembodied glow of a pipe. Gradually a shape grows around it: Richard emerging to fill the moment with unambiguous delight.

'Why did you run away?'

Why? Because my longing to be with you overwhelmed me; the shame of my naked hunger for you exposed in the dishevelled darkness.

'I – I needed to find myself,' I say. I went out in the rain and chased the moon from puddle to puddle, splashing in muddied waters, running like a bat out of hell until my heart raced because I was out of breath, not out of control.

'Had you lost yourself?'

Laughing, he takes my hand, and leads me gently back across the garden and out into the night. His fingers, twined in mine, trace my desire. Far off, a baby cries; and in the road, an abandoned dog yelps in pain. But this night belongs only to us. We leave behind houses, people, propriety. Holding each other's hearts, we cut through the darkness and marvel at this flawless new world, suspended on a breath between us. When the chrysalis is broken, we also shall be gods.

I dart through the undergrowth, my dreams galloping ahead, straining the reins of credulity. But you are not chasing me, and tears prick your eyes. 'You crazy beautiful nymph, come here.' And you take my face between your hands and give me that kiss which no amount of rehearsal could have imagined.

Then you hold me away from you and your words leapfrog in my ears: 'Dear heart, once I would have romped through the night with you, made love to you with intemperate passion till dawn. But now... I'm an old man, Danielle. Oh that I had met you ten years ago!'

I would have been nine years old, I think with irritating logic. And you can't be *much* more than thirty.

'Then I shall teach you to be young again: to be up before dawn to see the world erupt from sleep, to run barefoot through the woods and feel the earth quicken your blood, to swim naked on a summer night and sleep covered only in stars. Richard, I'll give you back your youth!'

'Ah, Danielle. You are so young, so – '

'So – what?'

'So young.'

Did you sigh then, or was it just the wind whispering cautionary rumours?

Memory maps the mosaic of that night with the gullible glow of innocence. An extended moment of perfection caught like a stop-frame on an old film, before the murderer is captured or the heroine dies of consumption. My recollections of it, recast by the rose-tinted wrappings of time, have given it a kind of isolated brilliance.

We hug the intimate coverlet of darkness more tightly around us, swathing ourselves in that moment's magic. A small stream stops us, rippling shyly as though it had lost its way in our dreams. Entwined in each other, we watch the night dance on the water; liquid longing, stars spilling assent.

Then the wind whips capriciously through the softness of the bourne and blows away my lover's face, and the disgruntled moon swims away in pieces.

You sit on a mass of ferns that yield unknowing to the one that crushes them. All ugliness rushes through the space that separates us. I come to you and cover your face with kisses. You hold me away. Was it only afterwards that I thought you were struggling to speak?

You kiss my eyes light as butterflies' wings and lead me back to the world of the undreamt. The stars go back to their appointed places. The night that had been exclusively ours returns to encompass the rest of the sleeping world.

*In the Beginning was the Word
And the Word was Love...*

Two

Memory is also moulded by things that didn't happen.

For three days we have hidden behind the polite exchanges of strangers. My mouth has dried out with the words I cannot speak and my shoulders droop with the weight of unused time. All actions, moments, other people, are clumsily irrelevant. I am consumed by this one huge want, which may be blind, but was never more incisively aware.

I ignore the present and hope that like an unwelcome party guest it will just go quietly away. But how shall I accomplish the bustling business of being, when all meaning crumbles through only one ungiven smile of affirmation? I conjure the night three nights ago when we swung the world between us, and wonder what I have done to offend him.

I stand outside myself and examine dispassionately the destiny that has entrapped me. Detached as a newsreader announcing distant devastation, I ask who could be ensnared there? He is not really handsome, his face is rough hewn as rock; he walks with a proud distracted air as though the truth of him were somewhere else. I laugh invulnerability, and return to my script. But when he bends towards me in a gesture of solicitude I am undone and curse that invulnerability was ever so false.

So I smile politely, trying to squeeze Love behind a tight mask of disinterest. He laughs, and turns back to the group, more favoured in their role than I. I lower my eyes, lest their shameless assault be transparent to even a casual onlooker. When I look up, I see only his back, flaunting indifference, and the space between us breeds no potent recollection.

My script weighs down my lap, unregarded as the moons that dare to rise and set without my acquiescence. And to muse upon him, only to muse upon him, dissolves me in tears of impotent despair.

Will no eloquence arise to save me from the clutches of his ubiquitous silence, and woo him back to arms that melt with longing?

* * * * * * *

Truth, it seems, if unpicked over-zealously, will inevitably start to contradict itself. But which is truth, and which is contradiction? Richard, opening his arms to me and closing his heart; wooing and withdrawing. A two-faced magnet. Truth, seen through the mis-shapen sieve of memory...

But work distracts with the call of the immediate, providing Pyrrhic salvation. Rehearsals demand my attention as well as my presence; the focus to go through the creative process, not just through the motions. Only now the theatre is busy providing answers to questions I have not asked. And do not understand.

All through morning rehearsals a kind of febrile anticipation informs my work, fed by my intention to rouse my reticent courage. At lunchtime I shall speak with him; I shall make him speak with me. But when we break at one, it is Croft who takes you by the arm, off to the pub for a 'working lunch'. And I sit brooding that I cannot metamorphose into a theatre director with a wild red beard and official claims upon your time.

And it is Vic who struts over to me, beaming his falsetto smile, come to stake his claim. But how, having seen Hyperion, can I consider the satyr?

Richard... You appeared at the door of the rehearsal room, trailing clouds of glory... Bemused, you stood there, a general mustering his troops, and everyone jumped to metaphorical attention. And when you smiled, bestowing benevolent bonhomie, everyone gathered round you, clamouring for favour. I waited, outside the circle, curiosity paralyzed by shyness. Later, you came over to me and without preamble you took my hand and said, 'You are not like the others. Walk with me.' Did you mean for life? Or to the café round the corner?

Vic, fawning to gain your approval, like a novice priest to his bishop, stops us in our tracks and loudly assumes the role of Company mouthpiece. With sardonic quips, he introduces each of us to you, saving his most saccharine barbs for me:

'Now Danielle, this voluptuous black-eyed Jewess, she'd be glorious in bed, don't you think?'

You undressed me with your eyes, seeing through my eccentric clothes the nakedness of my jangled emotions. Then, not taking your eyes off me, you said to Vic: 'There's more to Danielle than bed. Much more.'

Yes. To be more, is first to be.

So Richard, when?

* * * * * * *

Silence. There are many colours of silence. The satisfied silence as a baby's hungry mouth finds its mother's breast. The rapturous silence at the end of a performance of Verdi's Requiem, before the audience break into tumultuous applause. The silence of stones, breathing buried sounds. The stunted silence when a trapped animal's whinnying finally ceases. The red-eyed silence of darkness to a terrified child. The wounded silence of a dying marriage. The vast silence of the universe serenading the secrets of solitude.

The silence that devours me when you do not call my name.

* * * * * * *

Off-stage I'm a poor actress. In the days when my mind still served me, I smugly thought it was moral judgement that kept me from indulging in the games people play. Now I know it's only a lack of talent. But I'm young, I'm pretty, there will be other loves. And armed with this seductive lie, I force myself back into the process of becoming someone else.

But all is not well in this world of make-believe. Croft bursts into my dressing-room, a mad bull chasing the cow that jumped over the moon.

'For Christ's sake, Danielle, what precious Antigone did you dish up for us tonight? Where was the hardness in your voice, the "ugly willful pride of youth"? Glory child, you've just renounced the man you love in favour of heroic death. Don't sound so bloody tender!'

But don't you know that love and death are only divided by the flip of a coin. Only, death is surer.

And then Richard's eyes, soft and green as summer grass, are smiling to me through the steamed-up mirror.

'And would Danielle renounce the man she loved in favour of heroic death?'

So you heard? Croft was right, and I am mortified.

'My dear, you look ravishing when you are angry. And made to be ravished.'

I stare at the mirrored face smiling ribbons of question marks. But confusion knots my tongue, and my unspoken words, like Macbeth's "Amen", stick in my throat. I, too, had need of blessing...

* * * * * * *

My thoughts are all and only of you. But the world trespasses my consciousness, willy-nilly. My landlady informs me that she has 'had a turn' and strings up my conscience between a professional obligation and a human one. I call the doctor, I make my landlady a cup of tea, I arrange for a neighbour to visit. I do the things one does. Then I rush to the theatre, her voice mumbling in my ears: 'You run along, dear. Don't worry about me. Don't know why you do it though, working all hours, no time for boyfriends, and such *nice* girls as you and Susan...'

Nice? Oh yes, nice. *Susan* is nice.

The half has already been called. I try to sneak into the dressing-room unnoticed, but the stage manager, the backstage God with attitude, has a thousand eyes for seeing only misdemeanours. I apologize for my tardiness, but make no excuse. He fines me half-a-crown – the price of a meal out with Richard; but preferable to one of his sesquipedalian lectures.

And then your face, furrowed with concern, appears round my dressing room door.

So you do care?

* * * * * * *

To be more, is first to be. This phrase rattles my sanity with the urgency of a biblical prophecy.

So, tell me, Gabriel of the flashing sword, how do you atone for a sin of omission? Another's sin, forced on me by default. Turning the trusting naiveté of a nineteen-year-old virgin into a Tragic Heroine.

In Tragedy no-one is safe. Not the killer, nor the victim, nor the onlooker in the wings who happens to be standing in the arrow's path. A mismatched trinity of players, caught in a chance shared second and frozen in time. You are each equally innocent – and equally guilty. All you can do is play out your appointed role, alone in the wasteland of your silent sorrow.

So I shall play as cast. But don't worry, no-one dies of a broken heart. Not these days. Not in the middle of the twentieth century. There'll be a few tears, a little blood from the wounds you have yet to inflict. But don't let it trouble you. We must each play our part, rehearsed a thousand times in the ravages of the human heart. And I should be grateful, for mine, after all, is the star part; you are cast as the villain of the piece.

Tragic roles become me, you said. Like Antigone, I refuse to understand: that nice children don't eat out of every dish at once, or empty their pockets to beggars, or run in the wind so fast that they fall and tear their clothes. Later, you asked why I chose to live my life as a Greek Tragedy, courting suffering on a grand scale; as though this would buy me absolution. But it wasn't a question; it was a way of letting you off the hook.

* * * * * * *

I cannot sit still. I walk around the periphery of my life with a glazed look in my eyes, to camouflage my tears, to ward off all adjuncts of sociability. Round the corners of my vision, noisy actors slouch in armchairs, read newspapers, learn scripts. They smoke, drink tea, gossip, pursuing artistic struggle or seduced by expectation of self-aggrandisement. Or, just doing a job. And all the while, Richard's presence throbs like an electric current through the greenroom and my heart.

I look down at my neglected script. I struggle to learn my lines for next month's production, to grasp the thread that binds Barblin to Richard; to find fusion in the confusion. She, wearing my skin, will slowly go mad each evening on stage. *He* meanwhile drives me to madness each wasting night.

Vic, spurred by the humiliation of his bruised ego, saunters over to me. He calls my name as though it were a bad smell under his nose. 'Dani*elle*, you shouldn't mess with love if you don't want to get your hands dirty, if you can't bear to sully that pure little soul of yours.' Yes, Vic. Spite often speaks with more clarity than does charity. But we are truly hurt only by those we love.

Susan interrupts me in the middle of not learning my lines, and calls me to the telephone, that marvellous weapon of non-communication. And down the line Gerry's voice startles me out of my stupor. Gerry, my dearest friend. Tall, handsome, with busy dark hair continually falling over his right eye; with laughing lips, purposeful gait, serious hands. Gerry, who cares passionately about real people, as well as 'humanity'. He is a brave human being; he will change the world one day. He loves me.

I turn to find you watching me. Why do I feel the need to explain?

'I – I've just been invited to London for the weekend. By a Glorious Man.'

'Enjoy yourself.'

'I'm not going.'

'Why not?'

A Pinteresque pause, overloaded as a pregnant elephant.

'I've got a part to learn.'
His eyes laugh into a quizzical twinkle.
'Barblin!'
'Ah. Come and eat with me after the show tonight.'

And you take me to the "Inn of Happiness" and feed me sweet and sour pork and ambivalent smiles.

* * * * * * *

Ambivalent smiles. Masked messages. Hesitant hands.

My patience has evaporated like the truth of election promises. I can wait no longer, no matter which devils of duplicity may be designing my downfall. No ruinous knowledge can bleed me more than this ugly ignorance. So, where angels fear to tread...

I have prepared myself for you, my love, bathing my body in cool water, brushing my long dark hair till it clothes me like black silk. I have painted my eyes with longing and my lips with the rosy tinge of expectancy. Only my cheeks lack the rouge of bashful blushes.

There have been other times, other men, when, hands touching, lips meeting, wild caress, and then nearly, I have wanted, breasts aching, body yielding, soul untouched. I have been waiting for love for you love for you my love for this night love of you of love of you love.

For everything is you, is this moment spun to perfection with the gossamer thread of my girlhood dreams. You are the land rising out of primordial chaos, the gentle face of the sun spilling love upon the seas, the sacred songs that shine the stars, lighting up all human possibility. You are the tides of all love that put a waterway around the world, drenching the earth with rainfalls of longing.

But life is not the theatre, and has chosen a banal

setting for tonight's unfolding drama. Your landlady's sitting room smells of dreams unrealized and quiet desperation, the shabby greens and browns of a lonely middle-age. The curtains, faded and sagging like her long-unused body, are drawn against intrusion, against possible comfort. And you, king of the night, sit in the shadowed silence, smoking your pipe, watching me with tormenting patience.

At my demand, you kiss me. Your mouth is soft, hard, questioning; your hands send messages rushing to my nerve centre, warning of approaching conquest.

But it is your passion that you conquer, not the woman yielding to the touch of love.

'O Danielle, I want so much to love you.'

Want to love me? Your wanting dries my moist expectancy. *Want* to love me? Your eyes, your words, your fingers, did they all lie then? And what demons of delusion were your kisses and your smiles?

'Oh, my dearest, I do love you. Of course I love you. But – I must not; for your sake. For my sake.'

The room sinks in silence. The only sound, the ticking of the time-bomb of disaster inside my head. The only proof that I have not yet disintegrated. Oh, the sins of presumption, the ugly sterile sins of presumption!

And then it explodes, the fuse your eyes have kindled, and I am pierced through with the falling shrapnel of your words... Time ago, and a young struggling poet met a honey-eyed painter. She was strong and she was weak and she was beautiful. She dreamed his dreams and married his aspirations. And they loved, and they made children...

The silence shrieks with pain. Your name writhes in my mouth, unspeakable.

You rock me in your arms, tightly, drown my agony of sobbing in rich brown wool. You smooth my tangled hair. As though it mattered. But I am not strong and I surrender my life to the comfort of my gentle executioner.

'Hush little one. Not such despair. It's not the end of the world.'

'It's the end of my world.'

'Danielle, my darling. I have loved you since... But – but Anna...'

'She has a name? How dare you name her to me.'

And I flee before weakness and your hands can change my mind.

* * * * * * *

Outside, the night is black. Trees drip despair. Stars shrink, shuttered; the empty moon is mantled in death.

I fetch up in the blackness of the forest. Skeletal fingers wag from nature's grave-yard. Shadows shriek. The undergrowth trips me up, traps me in convulsions of despair. The forest flies apart, pistol-whipped by my cries. Leaves whirl; tornadoes of grief. Rusty mud squelches, cementing footprints of sorrow.

The charred sky weighs down the night with spectres of shame. Jagged branches, ghost arms, jump out at me, tangling my hair in webs of insinuation. Dead women's laughter rapes my ears. A lone screech owl records and forebodes disaster.

Bones crackle underfoot. Earth wounds, screaming menace. I run and fall, run and fall. Tripping over my desolation. Stumbling blocks of consciousness. I am eaten alive. Swimming in the belly of the whale.

The weight of existence crushes me. I bang my head on the ground to wake from this nightmare but the nightmare is reality and reality is Richard belonging to another and reality is the mutilated world toppled with regret.

Who among the angels, of God or Lucifer, will comfort me now?

In the Beginning was the Word
And the Word was Love
And you my love
Are the word made flesh...

Three

"The spring is wound up. It will uncoil of itself. That is what is so convenient in tragedy."

Playing Antigone has become my escape. But not my salvation.

"The rest is automatic. You don't need to lift a finger..."

'Danielle, darling, please. Don't run away...'

"Death, treason and sorrow are on the march; and they move in the wake of storm, of tears, of stillness."

'I tried to tell you sooner, so many times, but I... '

"Every kind of stillness... The unbreathable silence when, at the beginning of the play, the two lovers, their hearts bared, their bodies naked, stand for the first time face to face in the darkened room, afraid to stir."

'I love you, Danielle. I didn't want to hurt you...'

"Tragedy is clean, it is flawless... In tragedy, nothing is in doubt and everyone's destiny is known. That makes for tranquillity."

'Dearest heart, I have loved you from the moment your eyes first smiled questioningly into mine...'

"Tragedy is restful; and the reason is that hope, that

foul deceitful thing, has no part in it. There isn't any hope. You're trapped. The whole sky has fallen on you, and all you can do about it is to shout."

'The truth of my love for you is not altered by any other facts...'

"I said 'shout': not groan, whimper, complain... But shout aloud; all those things that you never thought you'd be able to say. And you don't say these things because it will do any good to say them; you know better than that. You say them for their own sake."

Richard, I love you. Too much to want anything less than all of you.

"The play is on... For the first time in her life, little Antigone is going to be able to be herself."

Yes. And Danielle?

* * * * * * *

In the far corner of the greenroom, I sit curled into the red plush armchair, a decaying relic from a pre-war production of "Private Lives"; worn and stained, but less frayed than my nerves. And I flex all the muscles of my concentration to speak with a voice that is not mine. But Barblin's lines do not stick. For my voice knows only one word, THE word, the word I dare not utter; for only to think of it makes my blood curdle and my head spin.

Richard, Richard, what shall I be without you? My body is turned outside-in with aborted desire. Long skirts and Indian shawls may camouflage my figure, but cannot hide my brazen yearning. Love, buried by the facts; single beads of unfilled moments, strung into a necklace that strangles hope. Lacerations of love, unbandaged.

And then he – the only he, the genesis, the seed – he, bursts across my vision. I cloak myself with fortitude, burying my vulnerability in its folds. But it is not resolution that glues me to my seat, but panic. Do you not see the havoc that you sow with your eyes? Your two siren eyes, milking mine across the day; drawing me through that sea of acute pleasure to my watery doom. Drowning in ungiven love. Oh the sharp merciless fingers of persuasion clawing at my heart!

I tremble at only his smile grazing the back of my head, and wonder with what fabric of self-deception I shall manage to clothe tomorrow.

* * * * * * *

I escape to the pub, that bulwark of British social intercourse, where joviality jostles for position, and drink scatters secrets like confetti. But it is no escape. The air is thick with images of Richard taunting me on every optimistic face that is not his. The mahogany beams, painted onto the wallpaper, mirror my fake reality. But loneliness is not choosy; it boomerangs off the walls anyway, knocking my fantasies sideways.

I wait at the bar busy with early evening drinkers, or people postponing their return home after work. I challenge Fate to believe that I'm one of the crowd, safe from her sadistic schemes. I order a pint of bitter, to drown the bitterness within; but it is no medicinal. There is no corner seat, and I am forced to sit in the middle of the room, clad only in an aching vulnerability, exposed like an ageing starlet to every juicy whim of gossip.

Two actors from the Company saunter into the pub, threatening sociability. They know that I have seen them and know that I know they know. But insulated in my suffering, I see no further use for my tunic of politeness.

I drink. I watch the world busy itself with its own

delusions. The clock on the wall ticks with pitiless precision, distorting with facts my flights of fancy. I wait until time has over-reached itself, then five minutes more, so that there will be no gap, no space, no unaccounted for moment, that Richard could intrude upon. Then I sprint back to the theatre, spurred on by the Furies spanking across my back.

But as I arrive at the stage door, jangled and out of breath, you are there, waiting to crush me with persuasiveness. My body tenses all its nerves, straining to hold the fear of not being able to stave off the one thing I most desire.

'Danielle, when will you stop running?' His eyes speak with unbearable tenderness, with puzzlement, with love. I escape to my dressing room and weep for the waste of life curling voluptuously round the edges of my dreams; I weep for my cursèd virginity that will accompany me too faithfully to the grave. But against love there is only one defence: to be out of range of its mortal weapons. And the world is too small.

* * * * * * *

Work ambushes my time, if not my dedication. And so at the appointed hour, I speak the excoriating words that Max Frisch has put into Barblin's mouth:

"Blood, blood, blood everywhere... I'm whitewashing, I'm whitewashing so that we shall have a white Andorra, you murderers, a snow-white Andorra. I shall whitewash all of you, all of you... "

But it is the blood of *my* wounds that gushes over the murderers of Andorra, the frozen anguish of *my* unfulfilled love, as well as my search for her dead lover / brother.

"Where were you, Father Benedict, when they took away my brother like a beast to the slaughter, like a beast to the slaughter. Where were you?"

I watch the terrible torture of Andri each night, and I do not know whose madness I whitewash across the stage: Barblin's – or mine.

"My hair ... will grow again ... Like the grass out of the graves... "

Yes. My darling, will you be there to brush it?

* * * * * * *

Richard is married. Richard has a wife. Richard has children. The words besiege my brain like a hell hag's inventory chronicling the world's disasters. I can synthesize no meaning. That is, the fact is clear, potent, and has been thriving, sickeningly, for ten years. But not why. Not how it stumbled into my life and is killing me. And it's the facts that will get us all in the end. My conscience contorts; thoughts, too, have consequences, rebounding with karmic venom.

So, what will be my prize for wrestling headlong with such despair? Can the scrivener, writing in tongues, offer absolution? Holy Texts teach of sublime love, but deceive with hypocritical ciphers, dancing over the graves of scholars. Unconsummated love paves no gateway to heaven. We use for excuse conscience, that indeed makes cowards of us all.

Richard, you held out to my unsuspecting innocence the apple of the tree of knowledge. There was nothing I could do but clothe my nakedness, and leave the Garden of Eden.

* * * * * * *

When I look up for the hundredth time from the script I cannot learn, I catch Martin looking at you, his limpid eyes reflecting my deepest desires. You walk towards him, confident as a teacher to a wayward pupil whose obedience he takes for granted. I rage at this betrayal, seeing my smile on his face met with such gentle collusion. In a better world, perhaps, we would all be guileless hermaphrodites dancing in the courtyard of love, defrocked of divisive garments of gender, where the prickly green fingers of jealousy could not grow.

But this is not a better world. I leave the greenroom with my shame; to find a quieter place to cry.

* * * * * * *

A two o'clock call disrupts my day-dreaming, and I plough my way back to rehearsals.

When we break, Richard passes me, and carelessly, or not carelessly, brushes against my breasts. My nerves prickle with desire, and anger that he should so casually abuse the protrusions of my sex. Humiliated as a disrobed nun, I try to hide the femininity that affronts me.

That has always affronted me. My tomboy childhood was more than rebellion against parental censure. It was my place, my birthright; wild games, shinnying up trees, muddied clothes; making fantasy wars, making real trouble. But adolescence overtook me, salient with shame and fury. My burgeoning sex irrefutably branded me, an outcast from the boys' adventurous world. An exile that coloured all future recollections.

'Did I offend you?' Richard's eyes are sardonic, but warm. 'Come and have a drink with me. Danielle, don't brood all alone.'

'No. And I'm not brooding.'

'Please yourself.'

But I didn't, at all. I go to the coffee bar across the street, familiar with foreign students waiting at table, waiting to unpack their lives. And I wait, alone; for the waitress, or for Godot – whoever will serve me best. I sit for an hour over one cup of coffee, diluting it with milk and tears, my fingers tapping idly, full of ungiven caresses. From the juke-box, the Rolling Stones scream out messages of mutated sex, and androgynous teenagers gyrate mechanically through simulated mating rites. How shall I survive without love in a world that overwhelms me with imitations?

It is not propriety that constrains me, nor pity, nor fear, nor altruism, nor even morality, nor the remnants of my own fierce conditioning; nor yet the knowledge that your longing, too, grows in its non-fulfillment. My constraint now is my need to write my side of our biography with the cowardly pen of correctness; my only defence against the Day of Judgement to come.

So, I wait. Time, in stilted spasms, unrolls the inevitable.

* * * * * * *

During the days, I manage to keep busy with the trivia that clutter my emptiness. But at night – at night no-one is safe from hallucinations of terror. Volcanoes in my stomach eruct the lava of loneliness. Sorrow splatters stymied stories among pink flowers on the wallpaper. Under their carpet of deception, the floorboards creak despair. My hair is shorn.

At the old-fashioned dressing-table mirror, a grotesque face mimics my misery; a face sallowed by weeping, and the debris of Barblin's make-up. It hounds me, lit up by half-mad eyes burning with impotence. I raise my fist and smash it into that face that launched my thousand sorrows. Tomorrow I shall buy a new looking-glass.

When I force myself to crawl between the cold sheets of my single bed, I know the exact confines of my loneliness. It drips from the walls. It hammers inside my head, a scratching virago, pitiless, unrescued. A menagerie of lusts cavorts through my flesh. Havoc jungles my body; a breeding ground for everything that crawls.

Time washes over me, stagnant, a shadow skin. The clock on the wall measures my desolation in half-hourly chimes. I doze fitfully, trespassed by your relentless absence. I wake exhausted, my cheeks and my thighs wet with tears of love. Sleep's leakage into waking world; reality mocking the imagination of dreams.

Another bleak dawn. I think of metaphysical death. It is an effort to remember to brush my teeth.

* * * * * * *

But Fate has been sorely tempted; decked out with the smiles of a duplicitous angel, she will win us with honest trifles. And blinded by love, we do not see the devastation behind her eyes.

A knocking on my bedroom door rouses me from fractured sleep. And you are standing there – an apparition that will surely dissolve if I open my eyes. But my eyes are open, brimming with sight. And you are standing there, in the flesh, your flesh, framed in the shadows of the doorway: Archangel of the night, riding moonbeams to enter earthly paradise.

Out of the darkness your voice calls to me and your eyes upon my eyes and your lips upon my lips make the coveted words I had fought so hard not to hear. I could no more have moved away from you then, than could the crucified thief have left the cross.

You lay me on my bed, and your hands sure and gentle remove my nightshirt and the last vestiges of my will against you. At last, at last.

Oh God, absolve me if this is a sin. But my heart

leaps and I know no sin was ever so exquisite.

"My beloved is mine and I am his."

And my body aches with all the ache of present joy and past postponement.

"I sat down under his shadow with great delight and his fruit was sweet to my taste."

And I open to receive my love and the throbbing darkness is spiked with stabbing pain with stabbing joy and this miracle of fire consumes us with its wild tongue flames. And our love is sealed in my red-hot virgin blood, upon your lips, upon my lips.

Then you cradle me in your arms, and kiss my tears of too much adoration. There is no more to give.

"Set me as a seal upon thy heart... For love is strong as death."

I could no more refuse
Your love
Than could the parched earth
The first rains
For I am the land...

Four

We found the cottage beyond the city walls. A safe house of enclosed moments. Refuge. In biblical times, places of refuge grew up outside city boundaries, where criminals or sinners, lucky enough to escape their persecutors, would be safe and untouchable by law. And we, with signs and symbols of shelter, have cloistered ourselves inside this cottage sanctuary, so defying the evil decree.

We clean out old memories hiding in crevices, cobwebs woven with whispers of secrets past. We make space for the cottage to receive our dreams. We consecrate it with love; love that the world defines as profane.

Reinterpreting the ancient Jewish tradition of inscribing sacred words of protection around our home, we paint the doorposts with Byron's love poems, and the gates with the "Song Offerings" of Tagore. We whitewash the cracked walls with hymns of joy to gentle Hymen, and weave our bedspread with wanton colours of a pagan love. It was not that we denied God, but rather that we found Him in places where He might have blushed to come.

Around the cottage, our private wilderness spits out a tangled riot of weeds, broken stones, stray cats; a few unchaperoned flowers struggling to push through the untended earth. For us it was Goshen, Arcadia, the New Jerusalem.

For *I* am the land, flowing with milk and honey, the leaping skies, the cloudless waves of the sea. I am all of nature, sown with the gentle seeds of love, and lie expectant as the first caress of spring, waiting to bring forth my fruit.

Love is sufficient unto love, claiming only its own fulfillment. What legend shall be born of this gentle prophetic act?

* * * * * * *

Tonight I weep tears of compassion for Anna. I know what she has lost.

* * * * * * *

"Rise up my love... and come away... for lo, the winter is past... the flowers appear on the earth, the time of the singing of birds is come... "

We walk across the fields behind the cottage, through the wood spiked with bluebells and the heady sensual smell of early summer, to the golden world beyond. Richard makes a small arbor from the stacked hay.

"Come lie with me and be my love..."

And I lie with you, covered only with your kisses and with stray wisps of hay dancing across my yielding body. And you give me, lying with the naked earth, that for which there are no words. Then you kiss my eyes full of love, full of tears. And I melt into the soft throbbing earth, into the prickling hay, into you. And

I float away across the valley, your kisses ribboned in my hair, only the taste of your love to fill my consciousness.

Then you lie resting on one elbow looking down at me, with love huge and gentle in your eyes. And my heart aches with a plenitude not to be borne.

When we wake, you watch me dress, and take my hand, and smile with me all the way home.

Love is strong as death.

* * * * * * *

A warm summer sun nudges me awake, pushing through the gap in the window where makeshift curtains stubbornly refuse to meet. The early birds have caught their worms; dawn has long since chorused. I open sleepy eyes and smile, remembering what we did last night...

But morning invents its own pleasures. Richard is at the Cathedral, speaking with men of God and other functionaries, and I am not called for rehearsals. I own all parts of this day.

I play at housekeeping, and beam the possessive on the fruits of my labour: scrubbed floors, washed windows, the huge weary mattress sunbathing on the veranda. And Richard's faded odd socks blowing salutations in the wind.

The warm air brushes me with endearments. Wood sorrel and lazy violets languish in the sun, damp breath of morning caressing new expectations. Richard's taste tattooed on my tongue, his smell braiding my hair; his presence nestling in the sultry whispers of the long grass.

The cottage smells of seared earth washed by summer rain, of emerging pride. I think of solid suburban housewives living their semi-detached lives, with spotless floors and plastic covers on their furniture removed only for visitors, their marital beds a tired status symbol that doesn't fool the au-pair. There but for the grace of God... Or Lucifer. But today I am touched with envy. This choice beckons me, tempting as a stranger one fancies strongly but fleetingly, knowing that afterwards there will be nothing to say.

I walk into town with love in my heart and two pounds in my pocket to spend. Skipping lopsidedly along the high street, my exuberance bubbles over into laughter. Strangers stare incomprehension at this Mad Woman of Chaillot, or hide embarrassed grins. For to laugh out loud, alone, is surely to be mad. But I was taunted for so long. The miracle wavered, shy and foxy, across the horizon of my dreams, just beyond reach. Now it is quickened, and I am flushed with power, and am as invulnerable and as coveted as Achilles' arms.

There is nothing now I cannot do. I can metamorphose at will: into a lady of good breeding dispensing hot soup and admonitory sermons to the city's poor; an evangelical miracle-worker, enabling the mentally crippled to throw away their crutches; a prophet, to beat swords into bridal beds.

Would you like some posy of love? A little daring, perhaps, or a song to sharpen your sensitivity? I have loaves and fishes to spare, and whole galaxies of good omens, specially gift-wrapped for the down-trodden and the damaged. I shall buy up all the sorrows of the world and bury them under mountains of amnesia. For *love* is the "new-born babe striding the blast..." There is no room, anywhere, for any permutation of any dimension of any object that is not part of this love. And there is no action so evil but that I should see in it only the good perverted.

But at the doorway of the butcher's shop I hesitate, petrified. Raw carcasses hang mute with the terror of their slaughter. But the butcher smiles without condescension, and I am resolved to break our virtuous vegetarian vigil [started, at Richard's suggestion, after I began to eat pork]. I buy a large juicy roast – and mushrooms and pimentos and sweet corn and good red wine. At home, I shall tease the man I love for his deistic claims that 'forbearance refines the soul'. But after dinner.

Back in the street, the crowds lure me with jostling amiability. But when I pass Woolworth's, memory is ambushed in the shop window, the haunted look in the glazed eye of my reflection jabbing me with shame, reminding me...

Then, Woolworth's was crowded with leering eyes staring through this trivial transaction to the core of my disgrace; seeing nightgowns and kisses and illicit whispers of love stamped across my crumbling courage. Compromise clothed me like a spotted disease as I fumbled to pay the salesgirl and escape. Outside, I set this cheap concession to respectability on my wedding finger. *This* was my true sin against love.

Between rehearsals and meetings with ordained deceivers, we tramped the streets, viewing trim little boxes where the rent was too high and the air too suffocatingly neat: the latest G-plan furniture *and* fitted carpets *and* real lace curtains to shield us from the gossiping eyes of neighbours. But all we wanted was four walls and an empty space that we could fill with each other.

Our nerves were shot through with restraint, with the weight of our hands that do not touch each other; with the antagonism of the world for happiness that breaks its codes. With wanting so little, which is yet everything. We chased time through revolutions of longing, and time was winning.

In the end, we find what we're looking for when

we'd given up the search; 'the universe' providing what the estate agents could not. It was Vic who told us he'd heard of a place out of town, proving hostility also to be fickle.

The cottage is dumpy, askew, neglected as a leprous orphan that no-one will touch. For us, it's perfect: the bedroom dominated by a creaky four-poster bed and our chafing imagination; the other room shy with faded ottoman, rickety table and three chairs, a brick hearth built on a slant, as though its blueprint were mapped with an off-key sense of humour. Along one wall, a euphemism of a kitchen: sink scarred with scabrous stains, cupboards with no doors, an ancient cooker still boasting remnants of the last supper.

Tongue-in-cheek [and in my mouth!] Richard carried me over the hearth. Home *is* where the heart is, leaking roof, cracked windows, flaking walls and all.

* * * * * * *

Our first Friday night in the cottage. I light candles and consecrate them, but not with the Sabbath prayers I learnt at my mother's knee. We bless the wine, we bless the bread: sanctification of millennia of Jewish practice; later, absorbed into Christian ritual. Transmutation.

You watch me across the shadows, your eyes smiling necessary affirmation. And when you kiss my irreverent lips, teasingly, and say, 'I think I could fall in love with a dark-haired Jewess with cocker-spaniel eyes and anarchic smile,' I am finally gratified that I did not metamorphose into a young blond homosexual actor, or a theatre director with a wild red beard.

Mother dear, forgive me my too blasphemous joy. I know that you wanted only my happiness – as you saw it. But the frame that you built for me out of your hopes and regrets does not fit the picture that I need to paint. And stubborn as vines that will not cleave to their supports, I have pushed your architecture all out of shape.

'You are far away?'

'I am here. But Sabbath candles... They're my childhood. My mother...'

'As long as she keeps her eyes closed!'

You move the candle-lit silence sideways and sing to me: songs of innocence, songs of experience; songs of praise and persuasion; songs of love. We could not have been closer had we grown together in the womb of God. And though by worshipping each other we may find our way to Him, I am happy to remain on the journey.

Our hearts spilling adoration, we make love, more with gentle laughter than with passion, with a sweet tender aching joy; with wonder. Melting into each other we fall, not into forgetfulness, but into remembrance.

Shadow dances across our naked bodies; flames circle upwards illuminating confirmation. Love reached through the body, but far far beyond the body. Flesh, weaving into spirit. Mystic consummation.

The moon undressing in our window. Stars mapped across your skin. Touching those places in you that my eyes cannot reach.

Hearts sewn together, bodies coiled inside each other's prayers, we fall together into that exquisite sea of peace, into each other's dreams, into silence soaked with sighs of sated longing.

The night turns softly in its sleep and embraces us.

* * * * * * *

In the fields behind the cottage, wrapped in the stillness of infinity, we feel only greater than we know. An opaque drowsiness lulls the air, a timeless quiescence between past and future. Space, inhabiting the mystery of silence; still life. Lying on the soft quivering earth, we ponder the colour of light; sculpt birdsong on invisible wings. We hold hands, and dream wordless dreams, and banish all thought of awakening.

Round the doorways of our vision, huge mauve and pink rhododendrons, a chance inheritance left by previous tenants, catch the early summer breeze. Wild pansies, campion, ragged robins, push out the horizon with rampaging purples and yellows, pinks and reds, hewn from sunlight. Carpets of bluebells pin down the fields. Today I truly see them; love, seeing the familiar for the first time.

Sky breath whispers in the trees, liquid air evolving into resonance of a Brahms lullaby; birds swoop, shaping sound on the wing. Eternity washes us with indolent sighs; musk of early morning kisses falling through foliage; earth's spill of love distilled in the slant of the late afternoon light.

Down in the gorse we hear a finch whistle, and see the first berries on the mountain ash. An impudent ladybird ambles across our legs; a buzzard swoops, remembering journeys to far away places. The air is restful, heather-sweet. Gold-red clouds lazily brush the sky with promise of a rain-free tomorrow.

Dusk comes upon us as a welcome guest. Flowers close their petals, birds return to nest; in noiseless ritual, nature fulfills her proper nightly ceremonies. Treading softly, we too take leave of our daytime dreams and embrace the night, folded in each other's arms, the world enfolded between us.

* * * * * * *

Early morning mist coils round the verges of my vision,

distant hills dissolving in light rain. I sit on the steps of the veranda, watching a wild rose grow, curling into contemplations of love. Living memories; distilling time.

Why doesn't the world go away, and leave me alone to daydream?

But it doesn't. Croft summons me to a Meeting before lunch, and I am rudely thrust back into the accoutrements of living. I am the naughty child summoned to the Headmaster's office, already guilty, though ignorant of my misdeed.

But as I enter his office, armed with contingent excuses, Croft is all smiles, and I am disoriented by this unexpected mask of conciliation. Only his desk stands massive and menacing between us, testament to past hostilities and the unequal balance of power.

I stand by the desk, transferring my weight from one foot to the other. I fumble with trepidation. I wish I smoked, to give myself something to do with my hands. Croft laughs, enjoying my discomfit, taking his time, and mine. He starts to lecture me on the value of the English Repertory System, the purpose of Creative Struggle, the Craft as well as the Art of theatre. And I know that I've failed on all counts. Fear grips my stomach; he's going to terminate my contract. But his eyes are smiling; and I realize that he's not sacking me after all, but inviting me to play Joan of Arc.

I try to match the harsh teasing edge to his voice. I try not to blabber platitudes of gratitude, or throw my arms around him in unprotected delight. I try not to let my thoughts fall out of my mouth: I am too young, too raw, too inexperienced. I try not to make a fool of myself –

He interrupts the confusion of my thoughts. 'Hillary is pregnant. You're my second choice,' he beams with teasing satisfaction.

I manage, coolly, 'Whose Joan?'

'Shaw's. And mine.'

I rush back to Richard with my news, unable to wait until evening. And he smiles his pleasure, and embraces my excitement. Why does this moment weigh less than the expectation that raced me all the way home?

* * * * * * *

On the outskirts of the world, we sculpt a landscape of merged memory. If we sculpt well, the land may learn to love us, too. We move rocks, heavy with time; kneading the spirit of place, shaping earth's destiny in our image. Like Siamese worker-bees conjoined at the heart, we hew and chisel and heave and mould, spinning webs of protection around our boundaries of grace. We draw blinds across the broken windows, across the draughts of the future rallying to blow away our precarious precious present.

'We' is my favourite word.

We lay down our tools and rest in each other; consecrating joined memories of the time before we met. A shared exile is as intimate as love.

And the cottage has learned to dream, too... "In the songs and silences of the night, in the sunlit smiles of dawn..." Moments of infinite conjunction, of future remembrance interrupted, held on a breath between us.

The cottage and Richard and love replete: talking in bed and making love in the hay, food out of tins and dry red wine, broken cups and mended hearts and cold baths when we run out of shillings for the meter. Candle-lit dinners, burnt saucepans, curious four-legged visitors. Inhabiting each other's laughter and stories and aspirations – love on an elastic shoestring. Writing our lives with each other's smiles. Gentle times, holding hands, listening to Beethoven or Bach.

We have become one flesh. One soul.

Almost.

Richard is writing a letter to Anna and the world has turned cold. I leave him alone with his words and sit outside, grieving. Future foreboding cramps my stomach. And although I know that this ugly moment will pass, I can see no way back to that island of time where we lay together in the long grass counting the steps of heaven.

In little more than three short months, ninety days – that in that obscene apartheid world that punishes the caring, would seem a lifetime – our stolen lease on happiness expires. Richard will stage his poems at the Cathedral, and return to his family across the Welsh mountains. And time, wooing us with winning wiles, moves fast or slowly, always in opposition to our will.

We have woven joined intimacies of music, painting, poetry; uncovered a shared vision of creative and spiritual pilgrimage. But one subject pounds my heart, incommunicable. I contort my conscience through hoops of hesitation; but the pounding grows louder, more menacing.

I gird my loins with courage; I shall dare to approach the king. Three times I prepare a feast for him. On the third evening, I have no excuses left. My request is only for information, and no-one will be saved by my actions. Least of all me. But I am driven by demons of desire that demand disclosure.

'Richard... I want to ask you something. About – about Anna. If – if as you say, you have exhausted all possibilities of your relationship with her, if you can see the end of your shared journey in your imagination, then – then what is left for you to manifest together?'

Your face dons a mask of unapproachable gravity; your silence beats me with brutish withholding. Finally you say: 'I am reminded of Pascal. "All the evils in the world derive from the fact that we are unable to remain quietly in a room."' And I cry.

Now you come out to where I sit hugging my hurt in the long spiked grass. Your hand is on my shoulder, my head turned away from you in shame at this green stain of love my face is wearing.

'Danielle, my sweet jealous child, I love you. And I will come back.'

I have to believe it. I believe anyway that at this moment you intend to. And so I push from my mind the hideous fear of the future, and renew my devotion to living this present which exceeds all superlatives.

You are the apple tree
In the woods
A fountain
Of living waters
Washing over me
A garden of
Endearments...

Five

I am inarticulate. I know only one word, THE word, the word that beats out the infinite rhythms of love. I am the watery womb of the world, birthing at last this miracle love. I am the oasis of all deserts, the breath of music drawn across the soughing sky, the ripe fruit of love come to term. And I lie weak-kneed on the trembling earth that is also waiting for your kiss of life.

I am not greedy. I ask nothing more from life than I have now. Only this intimate grammar of Now: the present perfect, the present continuous, in which the real experience of the human heart is carved. Moments that cannot be measured, cannot be held back, that will only slip by uncelebrated if we turn the other way.

And Now is everything. It is the waterfall of sunlight cascading across our bed in the early morning silence; it's the sunlight, our bed, the silence. Now is the first dew upon the waking earth, the robin on the window-ledge, resilience, your smile.

Now is an attitude of heart.

****

In the white glow of midsummer, images are fixed in the thousand eyes of the skin, glinting, dense with desire. The place we inhabit when we're alone together; morning smiles cracking open the new day.

We rush the thorny tasks of daily living, escaping the intrusions of tea-cozy gossip, and the fear in others' eyes. We stretch intimate hours of words in front of the cottage, stolen moments loving silently in the fields beyond. We carve a capricious tongue of land out of rocks of longing: wild roses in one corner, rusty cans in another; discarded fruit rinds mulching in the wilderness, walking away on ant backs. Languid, copulative air; an aching lull in time.

On the tumbledown veranda at sunset, we ponder the ascending layers of belonging. Richard peels an orange, the peel a perfect spiral; orange glow of dying day unwinding. In the way he peels the orange, I see the way he loves me. We eat the segments, surrendering to a soft shared silence.

'It is in the precision of silence that lovers reach closest to the truth of their love. For even the best-intentioned words may be open to *malentendu*. The lips of the one and the ears of the other own different interpretations.'

'My lips own only one interpretation!' I tease as I swallow his lips in mine.

'I should like to read you a few lines of my new poem. It's not finished yet, but –

"No beginning, no end,
But fullness and fading
In long Bacchanal,
A bowing on strung wires.
The song like water
Shot in oak knots
Deaf till pierced
And brought to love's light... " **

'"Bacchanal"? Connected to Bacchus?'

'Worshippers of Bacchus. The god of fertility of nature, also of emotional rites. Later, he became known as the god of wine and drunken revellers. Take your pick!'

'God of fertility is fine with me!' I sip my wine lustily. I hold Richard in its embrace, drinking in the taste of him in 1954 Chardonnay.

'Richard, I've wanted to ask you for a long time. How do you make poetry? I mean, what is the *process*?

He is thoughtful, choosing words with the sharp precision of a surgeon, cutting no more than necessary.

'You mould words from the language of the soul; carved from passion, recollected in tranquility. But all a poet can really do is warn.'

'Warn? Warn whom?'

'The philistines. Perpetrators and guardians of a corrupt and corrupting culture. The whole cabal of vested interests in Fashionable Art. They don't listen, of course. But... "Poetry shall tune her sacred voice, / And wake from ignorance the Western World". Samuel Johnson. One day.'

He pours me more wine, deep, dark, 'like the deep pools of your eyes. Woman, you are beautiful.'

'Only when I look in your mirror.'

'No. When I look in yours.'

He holds me with his eyes, penetrating to the core of me, seeing inside of inside, and still smiling.

'You have given me more even than profoundest love. You have uncaged my art, as well as my soul: creative and sexual energy feeding into each other. Riding the spiral of time. The soul and the flesh, the heart and the mind. Sun and moon in eternal circular dialogue.'

He pauses, runs one finger slowly across my breast, drawing me. 'I have never written better poetry than during these last weeks with you.'

And I have never made better love...

* * * * * * *

Daytime rehearsals, evening performances, nights of love and smiles. The shrill ring of the alarm clock breaking open our dreams, sleepy grunts and kisses, the daily severing hurt of facing the outside world. Glorious Sundays exploding with space to fill only with each other. Days driven by love.

The hurt of being alone on earth if you mention a name I do not know; small squabbles, buying the sweet taste of reconciliation. Naked bodies wrapped in one sleep; naked looks that ask the world, and give it back replete. "The pain of too much tenderness..."

Like the quality of mercy, I am twice blessed: giving what I have most yearned to receive. My love can ignite compassion across the world and, like the burning bush, never be consumed. Regret reimagines itself through the prism of my love. And guilt is dispatched with the unsung villains of literature, to the compost heap of history.

Do I offend the gods strutting in my brazen robes of gratified desire? I shall not apologize for being happy without the world's permission. For to be even moderately happy creates enemies; mediocrity disdains all miracles. Undeserving, I know, I've been singled out and offered the world on a silver platter; gratitude reinvents my generosity. I shall give away everything I have that was precious to me before: my new black leather coat, five pottery mugs, an original Kuhn painting of a fisherman, Good Looks.

I shall even forgive the sour pinched teachers who stole my childhood, and smile humility at the self-appointed wardens of my soul against whom my revenge was to be my own success. And I shall gather all the world's pity in my arms and lay it, like a pilgrim at the shrine of God, at Anna's feet.

For everything affirms this miracle hanging breathless across the sky: the kind glance of a stranger in the street, ripe fruit on the trees, the rough laughter of children freed early from school. I stride through the world with eyes honed open, but see everywhere only the light of your smile.

And you are everything: the early morning sun brushing sleep from the skin of the world, the sensual sea shoring up its songs, the night sculpting metaphors across the sky. You are the old oak tree where God sits and ruminates, birds gossiping in the hedgerow, flowers rebirthing at dawn.

You are a safe harbour after hurricanes of heartache.
Home.

* * * * * * *

'"You promised me my life; but you lied. You think that life is nothing more than being stone dead. It is not the bread and water I fear. I can live on bread; when have I asked for more? It is no hardship to drink water if the water be clean. Bread has no sorrow for me, and water no affliction. But to shut me from the light of the sky and the sight of the fields and flowers; to chain my feet so that I can never again ride with the soldiers nor climb the hills; to make me breathe foul damp darkness, and keep from me everything that brings me back to the love of God, when your wickedness and foolishness tempt me to hate Him. All this is worse than the furnace in the Bible that was heated seven times."'

'Word perfect.' He hands me back the text of "Joan". 'You know, it was a revelation to me this afternoon, watching you in rehearsal, transforming into someone else before my eyes. I could have fallen in love with you – if I were not already in love. With a sorceress!'

I kiss his laughing eyes. He disentangles himself and continues: 'You know, you have a magnetic presence on stage. Very powerful.'

'And – off stage?'

'Differently.' Your eyes smile their crooked smile. 'Theatre is a magical art, words beginning to breathe, taking on a life of their own. Transfiguration. When you get it right.'

'Yes. But that's so hard to do. So hard. To reach the truth of each moment. There's so much "smudging"; and abuse, in a way. Actors loving themselves in the Art, and not the Art in themselves – as Stanislavsky says more or less. It's not as creative as writing poetry!'

'Creativity isn't a commodity to be compared. It's a gift to be nurtured – and not flaunted.'

'But performance is only interpretation. Second-hand creativity. In the theatre you're speaking in someone else's voice.'

'No. You're speaking someone else's words. But in your own unique voice. The job of the artist – any artist – is not to reproduce the visible, but rather to make visible the unseen. That's what theatre does – when it works. All creativity is an act of love – and hard work!'

'And is all love an act of creativity?'

'Profoundly. Great love is the greatest work of art.'

'And you speak with authority?' Four eyes tease each other in the gathering dusk.

'Great authority. Would you like to test it?'

And I did. And he does.

* * * * * * *

Wrapped in the skin of time, we unroll the reams of the present; eternity folded back on itself. We quilt rainbows of longing to rouse the inertia of infinity… We muse together in this other Eden, sculpted from breath of wind, from joy too deep to hold. Filaments of light painting your face; luminance of love. Time tracing lip-prints on your back. Your voice, sultry as a slowly-bowed cello, breathing the trees. "Heaven is lying nearby…"

My fingers mapping the landscape of your body. My skin remembering the touch of your dreams.

I have been waiting my whole life to rest my head on your heart.

* * * * * * *

A warm summer Sunday. Richard sits on the veranda at the three-legged table – Pythagoras' table, he calls it – working on a poem.

I sit on the steps, with the text of "Joan" on my lap. I sit on the steps, watching Richard: the stoop of his concentration, the sweet exhalation of his pipe tobacco, his fingers twisting the air, shaping words. The way he sharpens three pencils and lays them out on the table in height order before starting to work. Details, growing into memories…

I pour two glasses of orange juice, because I'm thirsty, because I want an excuse to interrupt him.

'I won a competition for writing a short story,' I say diffidently. 'When I was seven.' He looks up, quizzical. 'The prize was a copy of "Black Beauty".'

'How nice.'

'How *nice?*'

'I meant, the prize was nice; unimportant. Not the writing,' answering my offended pride. 'What happened to it? The writing, not the prize,' he adds, twinkling his eyes.

'Well, I suppose I've always been a secret scribbler. Trying to work things out on paper. To – to uncover the unknown.' I run out of steam.

'Go on.'

'My cousin Jeremy is a successful writer. The "writer mantle" in the family was already taken.'

'And the real reason?'

'I can't sit still long enough!'

He laughs. 'Can that be the Danielle I know?'

'Writing was always something I'd come back to. When I was older.'

He flinches momentarily. I see in his eyes a reflection of me as a little girl. He will always be fourteen years older than I am. I can never catch up... It makes him feel old.

'Somewhere along the line, it got transmuted into acting. Theatre became my god.' Ante, ante... 'And I love everything about the theatre: the smell, the texture of the work, the process of wading into someone else's life.'

He watches me silently.

'But actually – How *do* you write? Is it only through struggle? Suffering? What if you're happy?'

'You don't create *through* anything. The work is its own directive. The work is the process; the journey towards, without thinking about arriving. Getting under the skin of the human condition, the tragedy, the stupidity, the despair. Being ready to peel off your own skin, to flay yourself alive, exposing your rawness, layer by layer. Like an onion. Not in order to display your nakedness, but rather to lay bare your flaws.'

'And like peeling an onion, do you cry?'

'Sometimes...' And he turns back to peeling.

* * * * * * *

Love is strong as death: empowering war-torn refugees, trundling boxes and bundles and babies across rubbled continents, to embrace new life; rousing a martyr's following, resculpting the history of a people; musing an artist to create a masterpiece. Rebirthing a body a thousand times in its arms.

Love: the word for which kings will abdicate their thrones, and milkmaids blush as they raise their petticoats in the hay. The word that spins my blood, as well as the orbit of the earth. Love: cracking open the ceiling of the world, seeping through the crevices of time.

But time is playing truant, and the price of our love will be extorted in future blood. The question-mark hangs like a crucifix over a pagan bed, unacknowledged, but immovable. And like sufferers from a terminal disease who refuse to admit that the future will live on without them, we close our eyes and implant ourselves firmly under the skin of this precious precious present.

But I am afraid; I have sown in joy, and now I fear tomorrow's reaping.

* * * * * * *

Cradle the seeds of love in your heart, my darling. Cradle the seeds of love.

* * * * * * *

Anger turns to fear as the clock ticks disaster with every passing second. Richard should have been home twenty minutes [twenty aeons] ago. He is lying in the road, covered in blood, unconscious, dead. I pace the floor, wrapped in terror, staring disbelief at the door that does not open to disgorge his ghost.

Footsteps on the outside path mock my panic; Richard's form looms lazily across my vision. And I rage, not at his death, but at his life spilling such banal excuse: a drink in the pub, 'unexpectedly' joined by Pete and Rosemary. Rosemary? That little whore, with lipstick smiles and bedroom eyes and hands that can't wait to grab hold of you. My face has turned green, and I am distraught that I am painted this other colour of love, breeding only sterility in the descending darkness.

Jealousy is cruel as the grave. Crueller; it is less final.

And then I am in your arms, smothering you with kisses and apologies. You hold me close and dry my tears and smudge a small smile across my face. But, my darling, you have created yourself a god in my eyes. Don't blame me if I don't hear the clatter of your feet of clay.

But oh, love, conciliation is brutally sweet. And I glow with the smug juicy warmth of your love inside me. And your kisses burn my tongue, and all my forbidden questions... Then your words skirl the darkness: 'Fuck you, you cunt, fuck you. Yes, yes... Bitch... Oh, yes, yes... You are the one... YES...'

* * * * * * *

The Opening Night of "Saint Joan": the performance melts all doubts and I know that I've made the right decision. The only decision. I have grappled with the gods, struggling to reach a coveted corner of grace, an epiphany that allowed me, in sudden inspiration, to become the instrument through which Joan could speak, neither parading my talent nor imposing my voice.

The Company bustle around me, effusive in their theatrical 'curses' and kisses and less or more grudging admiration. Even Croft gives me a bear-like hug and says he's 'pleased' with my performance. And you stand with me in the wings, quietly, and hold my hand, and all my worlds coalesce.

But soon they will be sundered: love and art in mortal combat, fighting the devil's duel across my heart. The unthinkable hours of the future are bumping into the present, an avalanche of time balls careering down the mountainside, gathering speed and their own destructive.

Croft agrees to terminate my contract at the end of the run of "Joan". And I relish, in small triumph, his reluctance. There will be time for work hereafter...

'Dear heart, you may regret it. Later.'

'Later doesn't matter.' How can it matter what I'm not doing when I am dead? 'Anyway, I can always go back... '

'But you won't.'

Richard, *you* are "the wind in the trees, the larks in the sunshine, the young lambs crying through the healthy frost, and the blessed blessed church bells that send my angel voices floating to me on the wind."

And it is without these things that I cannot live.

You are the Word
And the wisdom
You are the seed...

Six

Last night you loved me, and you said:
 'Love is a state of being; a direction....'
 Last night you said, 'Whore, open your legs.'
 Last night you said, 'Now we shall reach the Palace of Wisdom!' And you wrapped my nakedness in the lineaments of gratified desire.

This morning, you are still wearing the same sweet exhausted smile.

You open your eyes, squinting in the sunlight. 'Happy birthday, little girl.' And you kiss the tip of my nose and stroke my hair and rest on one elbow studying every part of me, as though to implant me in your heart forever. And suddenly, I am afraid: you are already creating memories...

I lie back, naked, and watch you watching me, your eyes weeping love, and I wonder how my heart can hold so much and not burst. I could not love you more had I given birth to you.

To-day I am twenty years old. I have never felt less like a little girl.

I close my eyes. For your birthday, I shall be up

with the dawn and paint rainbows of love across the cottage walls and lay all the world's enigmas at your feet, wrapped in layers of tissue paper and adoration. No, I shall not. You will not be here.

You get out of bed and bring me love on a tray – orange juice and toast and marmalade and coffee, and a wild red rose from our own private wilderness. And a small parcel.

'A present for you,' you say. And I say, 'I have all the present I want.'

I open the beautifully bound volume of Lao Tzu's "Tao Te Ching".

'I love you, Richard.' What more is there to say?

* * * * * * *

During the day, a dozen red roses arrive from Gerry. It makes me happy and it makes me sad. For one cannot love judiciously, choosing a lover because he is adoring, or deserving, or suitable. Or available. And close friendship may be the very thing that precludes sexual love: we do not fall in love with those with whom we stand in confessional relationship. We are naked; but without mystery.

Nor do I love Richard *because* he is forbidden. I loved him before I knew him. I loved him before I met him. I have been waiting my whole life for him to find me.

* * * * * * *

But Canterbury has other legends on its mind, sliding down the centuries, struggling for their moment of glory. The Cathedral towers dominate the skyline, raw bone jutting through the rind of the city, God's palatial residence chiselled into its heart. Inside, a maze of moderate magnificence protects God in this ritual game of hidden and seeker.

Now, in the Eastern Crypt in front of the Jesus Chapel, a raggledy group of twentieth century actors metamorphose into a medieval motley, costumed in rough clothes and borrowed virtue. We reread the last of Richard's poems, a medley of discordant voices magically mutating into a symphony of sound. One of the last rehearsals before Judgement Day.

On my gilded shrine of possessiveness, I sit draped in Richard's reflected glory. Even Croft, who is God in the theatre, only more uncompromising, has been dethroned, and shows me wary respect. Living with a married man, your liaison becomes a story told by others. I smile: in what contempt and what esteem I have been held, by the same people, because of my relationship with Richard. What idolaters of Baal we all are!

But all is not well in the Temple of God. Celebration, it seems, is turning to requiem. The priests, in their infallibility, have changed their minds.

'Mr Yates, this is a Cathedral. I'm sure no-one would object to your poems being read at the, hm, theatre...'

Richard's eyes grow dark with anger.

'Yes, I quite understand that the Archbishop has a monopoly on God.'

'If you could see your way to changing some of the, hm, slightly offensive lines...'

'Thank you, I prefer to remain a "heretic" and keep my poems intact. "The Vision of Christ that thou dost see / Is my vision's greatest enemy." William Blake,' he adds, as their faces glow with ignorance.

'Yes, well, it seems that we don't all appreciate Christ's teachings in the same way.'

'But that's the point of the poems, to make people *think* about God, to question...'

'Don't argue with them, Danielle. Good day, gentlemen.'

We leave the House of God in silent fury, cursing that hypocrisy should be clothed in such bright opaque vestments. The church may no longer burn 'heretics' at the stake, but it still brooks no dissenting voices.

'The frightening thing is, they didn't understand what the poems were saying, until the Bishop took umbrage at the "New Dream" and explained it to his acolytes. Dear Mother Church, I am sorry for your children. Danielle, dear heart, don't be anxious,' as he reads my worst fears before I've allowed myself to think them. 'There is still enough to keep me in Canterbury for another three weeks.'

* * * * * * *

Enfolded in each other's arms, we gaze up at the night. Stars, a million light years away, aching towards us in billions of heartbeats, illuminate the infinity of love. The sky weeps waves of wonder, curving away towards heaven's horizon; leaving us only night breath of old sighs. The moon on a sheet of water.

Enfolded in each other's arms, we are transfixed by time looking for itself in space; by the touch of shadows. The world swathed in swaddling clothes at our feet, we soar. The invisible pushing through the wind, moved by longing.

Spiralling through mists of mystery, I strain to reach the far shore of the night, yearning towards that ineffable stillness, that place of bliss beyond. But I am constrained by tightly boned corsets of mortality. Revelation, defeated by the weight of human flesh.

Oh fly, fly, Icarus! Step out of your legend, and let me touch the sun.

"The Prophet's" words flood through me: "And

when you have reached the mountain top / Then you shall begin to climb.".

I have reached the mountain top, the roof of the world. And Richard is there, waiting...

I wrap myself more tightly inside his skin.

Falling through space. Gravity, pulling down the stars...

* * * * * * *

Children's playful shouts greet us, and the barking of tamed dogs. Through the garden of apple trees and clinging vines, the house emerges: Richard's sister's house, neat and squat, as she is. Her face beams jolly smiles of welcome; her eyes look at me pleasantly, but are not home to any curiosity. I smile. I manage a firm handshake. But when Richard introduces me as a friend from the theatre, my stomach turns somersaults of indignation at this easy mockery of the truth. A friend from the theatre? We fuck every night, I want to scream at them; to jolt them out of their sweet smiling complacency.

On the terrace, we indulge in light summer conversation and homemade lemonade. Neither sparkles. A black and white kitten loops round our feet, fleeing the loving of the youngest child. Meg and Richard share uninhabited smiles. She makes polite efforts to draw me in to the conversation; she tells me about the church fete and her oldest son's prize for woodwork. She asks uninformed questions about the theatre in a voice of gentle unconcern.

But when her husband puts a proprietary arm around her shoulder, the weight of your arm that is not around my shoulder crushes me from a distance of five feet. I am extinguished.

And Anna dominates the conversation, an absent saint to whom all are paying homage. Meg sings her praises in prim cathedral voice, crashing syncopated defeat into my frail illusions, and Richard makes the necessary excuse for his absence from the family home.

But he isn't with Anna because he's with me; he's *living with me.* He's my lover. It's my kisses that keep his blood circulating, not Anna's pained wifely smiles. You've got it all wrong, you nice, contented, dull family family.

But it's *your* apologies that annihilate me, your cowardly eyes that steadfastly refuse to answer mine.

I am a country bumpkin come to feast at the Squire's table. A tortoise, shell-shorn; pilloried. Why have you brought me here? To show me the family to which I will never belong? To have a voice of adulation sitting at your feet, praising the brilliance of your poetry to these people who do not understand it, and deride your need to create it? To show me that the world you inhabit belongs to Anna, not to me?

Or perhaps to show off, that you have 'talented' young friends in the theatre who admire you? To use me to give legitimacy to your work in Canterbury, to justify your absence from home? Well, my dear, I shall justify it; but not for this. And I shall not withhold my looks, burning with possessiveness.

The conversation limps on: their work, their parents, their cousins in Canada. But when it turns on children, I fill my ears with deafness, and my heart with lead. I am an outcast, beyond the pale of this intimate family circle, defined, contained, reduced, by this nice tweedy ordinary older sister, and Richard's tame acquiescence. And when we leave, I know that it is Anna who will have the last laugh – and I the last tears.

From the bus stop we walk back across the fields, and Richard is overflowing with gestures of love. But his kisses brush my lips with the bitter taste of recompense. And though my feet walk in perfect time with his, my heart is beating to another truth.

A swallow shrieks across my vision, swoops downward, then darts out of sight. The grass begins to whisper. There is a dampness in the air; soon the last cerulean skies of summer will fade into the brownness of tomorrow.

* * * * * * *

Richard sleeps the sleep of the innocent. I cradle his head on my breast and caress his cheek and watch the gentle ebb and flow of his breathing. Oh my darling, give me excess of your love, that I may arm myself against tomorrow's slings and arrows. But your love can know no excess. And if I try to build a storehouse to fortify myself against the lean years of the future, then like the manna that was gathered in the wilderness, today's portion withers as tomorrow dawns.

Oh my love, hold me, hold me. Suddenly, I am afraid. The time for such a word is creeping up on us from day to day.

* * * * * * *

Drinking rough country cider on the tumbledown veranda, we read to each other from Yeats or Pound or Blake:

"'This life's dim windows of the soul / Distorts the heavens from pole to pole / And leads you to believe a lie / When you see with, not through, the eye.'"

"'Land of heart's desire / Where beauty has no ebb / Decay no flood, / But joy is wisdom / Time an endless song...'"

We use words of the poets to indulge love; we use words of the poets to hide behind, to mask our fears. To keep our eyes on the page and avoid seeing in each other's faces the immutable dread of the future. We use the words of the poets because our own words are worn out, or too heavy to raise; or because the words that fall from our mouths name other things.

Remember, I tell myself as Richard locks his fingers into mine; remember this hour, when you held the quivering world between you. Remember it, when you will have only moon memories to feed upon. And I accept it open-mouthed, knowing that nothing, not love, nor bribery, nor pity, nor desperation, can ever give me any tomorrow. And in this vulnerable moment, on this warm summer night, I am happy to give everything, knowing that what I hold between my arms is all that I will ever be given. Is enough.

* * * * * * *

Today I planted chrysanthemums. They will flower after Richard has gone.

* * * * * * *

"Rise up my love... and come away... for lo, the winter is past... the flowers appear on the earth, the time of the singing of birds is come... "

We walk across the fields behind the cottage, through the wood spiked with bluebells and the heady sensual smell of early summer, to the golden world beyond. Richard makes a small arbor from the stacked hay.

"Come lie with me and be my love..."

And I lie with you, covered only with your kisses and with stray wisps of hay dancing across my yielding body. And you give me, lying with the naked earth, that for which there are no words. Then you kiss my eyes full of love, full of tears. And I melt into the soft throbbing earth, into the prickling hay, into you. And

I float away across the valley, your kisses ribboned in my hair, only the taste of your love to fill my consciousness.

Then you lie resting on one elbow looking down at me, with love huge and gentle in your eyes. And my heart aches with a plenitude not to be borne.

When we wake, you watch me dress, and take my hand, and smile with me all the way home.

Love is strong as death.

* * * * * * *

Only disaster rings the doorbell at six in the morning. Richard buries himself more deeply in his dreams. I throw a coat over my naked drowsiness and shuffle towards my doom.

'Sign here, please, miss.'

I sign, my life away.

I resist the impulse to burn the future that is surely imprinted here and scatter the ashes in the wind. Dazed as a sleep-walker, solemn as a prize for effort, I crawl back to bed. Richard pulls me to him under the blankets. As though the world were still intact.

'What was it?'

'A telegram. For you. Here. What is it?' As though I didn't know. But not the details. Not the actual words of my death sentence.

'Anna has been taken to hospital.' And then the shortest pause that ever divided lovers. 'I shall have to go back.'

Six words on a small scrap of paper, and my world has crashed. This moment that too much dread has torn to shreds, has pounced upon us and caught us off guard, our brief for the defence too brief, full of flaws. How can this shadow woman steal twelve days of my life? Twelve nights.

You look at me crucified, one hand nailed to Love, the other to Duty, your soul splayed in the ravages between. I hold you in my arms to comfort you, to comfort me. But you are already withdrawn, claimed by the railway timetable and future implications.

How simple everything is when there's nothing more to be done. ["The spring is wound up; it will uncoil of itself..."] Time has accelerated, and arrived like Mephistopheles to drag my lover away. And it is not one crumb of consolation to know that he returns to her out of duty, or pity, or guilt. He returns.

We sit quietly, drinking coffee, watching the second hand race itself around the clock. We are calm now. The tears are already cried; they will soak all the days of future desolation.

"Tragedy is restful; and the reason is that hope, that foul deceitful thing, has no part in it. There isn't any hope. You're trapped. The whole sky has fallen on you." I play out my final curtain, rehearsed a thousand times in the terror of my nightmares. But someone has stolen my props.

I find a treasured copy of the 'Rubaiyat of Omar Khayyam'. I give it to Richard. For Anna. I am cursed, it seems, with great dramatic flair for the misplaced heroic gesture.

From the bus stop, we walk the short distance to the station, slowly, holding hands, reinventing these last moments of grace. Afterwards, you said you knew I would be strong. But you're cheating: *afterwards* is the crisis. I am not strong. You have painted the brave face I wear, and it will disintegrate the instant you remove your mirror.

The voice of the station announcer stabs through my cracking heart. It is time.

Richard sags into the train. He lowers the window, as though this were what separated us. His eyes bleed with sorrow. But no matter where the journey takes the one, the greater hurt is always left behind.

'Danielle, be brave. I will come back. Will you stay on in the cottage?'

'Yes, I'll stay.' And wait for you. Till time disintegrates.

'Bye, little one. I love you.'

I hold back the tears until the eleven-o-three train is no more than a speck of dust on my crumpled horizon; then I weep tears of all anguished humanity. Pockets of wars may be raging across the world, and graveyards deform half Africa with the detritus of man's obscenity to man, and the wailing of bereaved wives and mothers rocks babies to sleep across three continents. But this moment bleeds only for me.

Two passing porters tell me to 'cheer up, love, he'll be back.' As though their telling would make it happen. They wink, but without malice, and bring me a cup of tea; the world intruding to postpone the future's blood.

I pick myself up from the box where I'd collapsed, to search a quieter place to grieve. But the world is too small. And Echo, like a mourning shadow, stalks me with lamentations.

My feet drag me along, obeying laws I no longer understand. This moment that too much fear could not postpone, has finally caught up with me. And like childbirth, all the correct preparations are irrelevant when the pain and the tearing overwhelm.

My feet have stopped walking, but I do not recognize the cottage. It has turned black. I see only the scaffolding of absence. Lucifer, open your gates! I hadn't wanted to fight with God, but anyway I've lost. My golden wings are burnt.

Richard has gone. And I am left behind.

Zeus is wooing Leda
What chance did I have
To avert the cataclysm?
My swan-song
Is of a different kind
And I sing
Out of tune...

Seven

God, come out of hiding and comfort me. Show me a way to endure.

My heart is cut out of my body and limps away, still beating. I follow the bloody trail and realize that I'm dead. But who will come to bury me, or incant eulogies by my grave? And who will be proof against the ghost in the flowerbeds, holding betrayal like a time bomb in its sightless stare?

The world is flooded over with rivers of my grief, washing away all innocence in the deluge. The dove has flown the Ark, but finds no resting place for the sole of her foot. And I have forgotten the taste of the olive leaf between my lover's lips.

How shall I stop from drowning in the river of tears cried at Marsyas' death? I challenged only another mortal, but her victory has flayed my soul. For it is *her* arms that enfold you when you wake troubled in the night, *her* vapid smiles, not my fresh aching kisses, that you hear lowing to you across the impotent darkness.

Guilt will copulate with loneliness, and remorse will be the midwife. But what shall be born of this savage unnatural act?

****

The grave of love lies cold under my blanket of deception. My bridal shroud swathes me in bandages of grief. And round my neck, the chain he wove out of beads of stolen kisses...

Where are you now my love, my heart, my knight in borrowed armour? Galloping across the Welsh hills on the back of resolution? Weighed down with deserter's medals, glinting in the sun? Redefining the ragged edges of responsibility, puffed up on your pillows of self-righteousness? Wearing a sanguine smile that expects a prize for good behaviour.

Are your nights not tormented by subversive memories of hay-blown passion? Do you not weep with forgotten sighs for that sea of peace you will never reach without me? Where now those angel days that we quilted together out of rainbows of desire, sewn with the sinews of our skin? Have you reached the other shore of Lethe without looking back even once?

Duty, like a beggar child, claws at the hem of your nightshirt, and drags you off to bed with perfidy. But though you sinned for Pity's sake, your sin corrupts Love. And is no use to Pity. Was it for this I surrendered my life?

God has it wrong. He didn't create me in His image; you have created me in yours. And I exist, even in my soul's secret places, only in your affirmation. How shall I live without your smile to recreate me? Or your hands to assure me that my body is not dead? Only the chasm of my loneliness looks back at me from the mirror of your time-blind eyes.

The price of remembering: in my bones. I am a caged bird, smelling the memory of summer. The longings of centuries ruffling my wings, crashing against the bars of my prison towards the sun, that only my ancestors have known.

I can only cry to you out of a small empty space that was once a woman that was loved. There is nothing left of me now except this cry. Except this cry. *De profundis.*

O love, love, love, amor immortal... Witches were burnt at the stake for less that this.

* * * * * * *

I walk to the village to give myself something to do. As though changing the landscape will change the hurt.

The village shopkeeper wears a gossiping smile, bloated as a plumped-up cushion; his fulsome lips wet with questions. But my eyes are painted blue to ward off all curiosity, camaraderie, comments; to ward off the Evil Eye.

I buy bread, cheese and an apple, to tempt my appetite back from the dead. I buy only ten cigarettes and an excuse to return later in the day. I have started to smoke so that I have something to hold onto lest the Moment, hovering at the edge of the circle, catches me unawares, with no simple action to root me in the world of the living.

I dawdle back. I take the longest route. To postpone my arrival. To keep future terror at bay. But at the cottage gate, the future lurches up to threaten me, a guardian Beelzebub at the entrance to Paradise, with flaming sword in one hand, and executioner's axe poised ready to strike in the other. He is wearing your face.

Seductive as the first snake, you coiled curiosity around my heart. Now I shall never reach the tree of life.

* * * * * * *

Down in the couch grass the wind torments the bracken. A lame sparrow scratches out her tuneless autobiography. Honeysuckle wear slippery smiles, wood fern chortle insinuations in the wind. White berries on the trees are stained dark crimson with my blood.

Wild foxgloves and lungwort defiantly turn their faces to the sun, insisting on growing without my consent. Rocks, knotted with deafness, sweat menace from open pores. Your footprints on the earth, tracing midnight moorings; your feet long gone.

A cortege of wild flowers attend my mourning, drooping in silent sympathy. The graph of my grief is drawn by the flight of a single swallow. The horizon hems me in, serrated with sorrow.

The day lashed with memory... How shall I find my way back to that armful of days in the sun, when we lay together in the long grass pondering the colour of wind? Or counting, on star light nights, the ascending steps of the moon?

Your absence tasted different when I knew you were coming home for dinner.

* * * * * * *

I need a plan for survival. To convince the angels that I still inhabit the land of the living. To convince myself.

A game of chess, perhaps, to challenge the gods. But it is Bergman's "Seventh Seal" of Death, black-cowled with menace, that materializes as my opponent, eyeless sockets taunting me across the board, waiting... I am a pawn in someone else's game. Now I shall never reach the eighth square. Or mate the king.

I shall try algebra; but I no longer know how to solve simultaneous equations. History bleeds only my regret from its wounds. Geography has split the world in two, and provides no map to guide my steps across the schism.

Literature tempts me with luring lies of the imagination. But its texts are irrelevant, the devil's deception. All books lead me to "Remembrance of Things Past". Words dance across the weight of my eyeballs, and all letters spell your name.

What of psychology, that marvellous modern malady for deciphering the dysfunctions of the spirit? But meddling mind mechanics cannot rationalize love, nor anaesthetize the vagaries of the human heart.

That fulcrum of civilization the Good Book, scripting all necessary codes, shall surely be my salvation? But wise maxims breed no solace: I want and I waste. I shall not speak with this Judas.

Necromancy then; the black art. Yes! I would willingly sell my soul to the devil for seven years with Richard. For seven hours. But without my soul how should I love you? Anyway, it seems the devil isn't buying souls today.

There can be no plan for survival. The paper philosopher has no truck with love. He doesn't know the cost. And I shall not be seduced by the lie of perspective. The doors of perception are clanged closed.

* * * * * * *

Time, from every fissure, eructs despair. Stones, carrying the weight of human suffering, are too heavy to be moved; except by silence.

Sitting in this wounded landscape, I lift up my eyes to the hills; but the psalmist unwinds my faith. Betrayal spills down the slopes; loss, chasing love down mountains of my grief.

The earth ruptures, drags me down. The dark descent into the underworld of love. But you looked the wrong way; now I shall never see sunlight again.

I postpone my life. I have no time for it now. Later... First, I must re-arrange the broken stones in the flower-beds. First, I must recite Blake's Songs of Innocence to the unsuspecting weeds. First, I must name the gods who sit mocking me in the branches of the old oak tree.

But Later creeps up on me, a violent intruder at a tea-party at the Ritz. I am finally caught up with. But one-eyed Fate with sadist smile refuses to arrogate my death; only my life. And remembering Juliet, I comply.

Nature, bristling conspiracy, mocks my mourning. The smallest ant, with solar antennae, can avoid crushing boots stomping through the fields. The lowly worm, dissected by jutting rock or malevolent school-boy, regrows itself twice over. But who will heal my riven heart?

Comfort me, comfort me, oh moon, oh waste of summer smiles, though Babylon is fallen, and all wars are lost. Comfort me. Give me some remembrance of yesterday; of that hour, in that night, when time held its breath, and his kisses illuminated all of Milton's vision. Remind me of the hour when I was brave.

God, wrap me in the panoply of your mercy and comfort me.

* * * * * * *

The theatrical world of make-believe abducts me each evening from this world I am trying to make believe. And twice on Saturdays.

The first rule of the theatre, invisibly impregnated across every Equity contract: the show must go on! I am dead inside, bleeding loneliness from every orifice. But the show must go on.

I go in early, but not too early; not to admit to the Company the extent of my misery. But I see no pity in their collective eye; only a faint mocking incomprehension.

Martin has befriended me. We have become accomplices. Like two abandoned impotents supporting opposite sides in some distant war, we are the only two who care.

It is the last night of "Joan". And Richard is not here. On Opening Night, you stood with me in the wings, quietly, and held my hand, and all my worlds coalesced. Now they are sundered, scattered like broken stars spit out of an angry sky. Why aren't you here? Seduced by Duty, you gamble Love's only future on Satan's gaming table. And Satan always wins.

The actors chatter around me, the usual buzz of last night ambivalence. I fancy I see smiles of kindness on some faces; but perhaps it is only smiles of condescension worn by those who understand this world better than I. In their rumbustious voices, I hear only your booming silence; a millstone round my heart.

Susan, wearing her niceness on her sleeve, clucks over me, like the nurse she played in Antigone; still wanting to help, still understanding nothing. Is it better to have loved and lost? It is better to have loved and loved.

Scene VI: The Inquisitor begins his interrogation. Heresy, Arrogance, Presumption. Violation of the sacrosanct authority of the Catholic Church. Sentence of Death by Burning at the Stake. I shudder with fear.

Joan's life is a tragedy of epic proportions. But it is simple. Cause and effect.

In the Epilogue, Cauchon asks, "Must a Christ perish in torment in every age to save those who have no imagination?" And will this death save the world? Save one soul?

Warwick speaks of truth as "political necessity…"

The Gentleman informs us that "the Church calls… Joan to the communion of the Church Triumphant as

'Saint Joan'."

Me. Saint Joan.

The Executioner says of her: "Her heart would not burn; and it would not drown…"

Her heart? And my heart?

Joan closes the play: "How long, O Lord, how long?"

How long…

* * * * * * *

I am not cut out to be a female saint. Celibacy festers across the wound of my sex. I am devoured by a jungle of lusts. A wolf gnaws at my nipples, howls obscenities at the door of my sex. A lynx eats my heart; a bat scrambles my insides out. Leeches suck at my breasts, hung like gaping mouths across the blood-red darkness, screaming for your lips. Tigers, smelling blood, savage my writhing flesh.

I am not cut out to be a female saint. If I am to be condemned to a monastic life then, like Heloise, it will be for my lover's sake, not for God's.

* * * * * * *

Dawn breaks around me, with a casual shrug of the shoulders, offering no magnet of temptation. I open my eyes. I am not rested, but am less afraid in a vertical position. I throw off nocturnal terrors with the bedclothes, and face the wounded silence of the day. A forty-watt sun grins sheepishly, poking slyly through the gap in the curtains, disclaiming all responsibility to provide light or warmth.

I go outside. I cross this wilderness of dead things to keep a rendezvous with memory. But *her* image emerges to demolish me, at once piteous and triumphant, dancing across the corn to seduce me with profligate tears of pity. Her face hangs on the wind, blowing through my seven veils of protection the wrath of Judgement Day. I see her gather blackberries, and hear her children calling to her across the meadows of my grief. Her honey-coloured hair falls long and limp over her gaunt angular breasts. Her eyes, half-wild half-sad, stare through the mist, bleeding accusations like a haemophiliac.

It is for *her* the angels will weep, not for me. For I have offended heaven. Her hurt gushes silent martyrdom, and bathes the earth with smiles of morning glory. I ooze only this septic pus of loss that drowns my soul.

My darling, don't you hear me calling in your dreams?

* * * * * * *

A loud knocking at the door rouses me. A uniformed hunch-back messenger thrusts an envelope towards me, then retreats with shuffling steps and inaudible mumblings.

A single sheet of paper, typed:

'My dearest,

'Forgive this moiety of a letter. Anna has been in hospital since I returned and preoccupations with the family have robbed me of all my time and energy. Anna has given birth to our fourth child. She is not too strong and ...'

Anna? Anna? Anna has...? Anna? No. Anna has given...? No. No. NO. NO.

Dear God, how can such anguish arrive so casually in the middle of breakfast? I was all filled up with pain before, where shall I find room for this new pain, so stealthily disguised in a small brown envelope? Written in the blood and tearing of your new child's birth. *Her* child. *Her* blood. Tearing me.

IT has happened. The end has caught up with me, found me out, crouching behind my mask of invulnerability, down in the spiky gorse. The apple, rotten with knowledge, half eaten. There is no way back.

SHE has opened her legs and disgorged a truth as irrefutable as the dizzy hurtling of this fiery planet towards its own destruction.

My heart bleeds, beating with the poisonous rhythm of the truth.

Have you forgotten
The oath
We swore to each other
Your lips
And my lips
Limed together
In my red hot virgin blood
Seeping up
Through
The miracle
Darkness…

Eight

Waking, I am beyond pain. Beyond tears. Desolation rattles my skull. Skin pulled taut with numbness. A ghetto of grief.

Knowledge rapes me. It roots itself in my guts. Propagating its poison. Cells dividing in malignant multiplication. It bloats my belly, but I cannot vomit it up.

Is there no way to sever the arteries of knowledge? To reinforce the illusion that what is not stated does not exist? The facts have not changed. Are not changed by my knowing them. But their satanic power has robbed me of my last hiding place. And who can remain innocent, accosted by knowledge: the obscenity of lives mutilated by poverty; limbs that walked and touched and loved, swept up in the rubble of a land-mine; children staring through starving eyes towards salvation that will never arrive. The world plundering metaphor for wicked justification.

I am the mangled mouth of the wound, the martyr sacrificed on the altar of expedience. For while we were making the earth move in Canterbury, your love inside *her* was waxing towards its fruition. In the battering of this ruinous knowledge, I cower like a cornered fox. Shall I now be forced to rewrite my diary of devotion? Recast memories with another's pen? Where is my place?

The duplicity of history; truth, stealing the past.

She has opened her legs and hatched my defeat. But it is *you* who are guilty. You, bludgeoning my brain with betrayal.

J'accuse.

* * * * * * *

But time and the faithful postman divulge another truth. I take his offering, invisibly stamped with love from across the Welsh border. A moat of memories, not yet lived, surges round my heart.

Perhaps we shall yet create the future out of our biography of longing.

'Beloved Danielle,

'It is now evening, and I write to you by the light of the oil lamp. I make words to you, and wonder, how will you receive them? Nearly two weeks have passed since we were together, and I grow anxious to know how you are. Dear heart, why no word from you?'

Why? But what in God's name can I write to you? Or in mine. I have no words for your new child's birth.

'And forgive me, my love, for those things you do not yet understand, as I forgive you for making judgement upon me. And perhaps, in the fullness of days, you may come to judge me less harshly too.'

You are right. I do not understand. I pull the alphabet apart, letter by letter; a child pulling wings off flies. There is a tear in every sentence, weeping words I can not unravel.

'Here there is much work to be done. The garden is overgrown with weeds, the house needs constant repair;

a ruin temporarily vacated by the birds, but not by nameless crawling creatures. Spiders rewind coils all year round on loose walls.

'I mind the children in the daytime [Anna is not yet strong]. Today they made houses in the heather. I walked to the cliffs to watch the sea: the long sea relentlessly grinding the pebbles. And your image pervades me. I see you strolling there and there. I take your hand and walk with you to find the goats – quiet sane creatures, blissfully unaware of the vicissitudes of human life. And I show you how to milk and watch you laugh as the warm liquid splashes over your arm and breast.

'Dear heart, it is hard for me here – '

It is hard for you? Then be resolute! Stop hovering between our three most imminent deaths. Commit one murder, finally. And come back to arms that melt with longing.

But I cannot write this to you. For you, with foxy foresight, have planted me on the moral highground. I can only gaze regretfully down the hillside at my runaway resolution.

But neither can I write, Make of me the sacrificial lamb, and stay with her. So I swing with the enigmatic world, strung up on the gallows of your indecision, of my pain.

'Dear heart, it is hard for me here. And I am here as it were on sufferance. So much time taken up with seemingly fruitless tasks. Though of course all tasks diligently undertaken are the work of the soul. But meanwhile my own work piles up, orphaned by the daily struggle for our survival: four young children living in this apology of a house with no electricity, so that performing even the simplest of tasks becomes hard labour. Certainly no leisure to ponder time's purpose, or read neglected masters among the dirty dishes!

'Yet for the while this is my place. And so I struggle, and so I work. It is the only thing. And pray that I may yet reach the young and still living, the strong of will and sensitive of spirit, that they may relearn thoughts, words, gestures; so that all received images shall perish, and honest work be the only goal.

'But I forget myself. For to whom do I write this: to you, my dearest, who know, and can distinguish the true from glossy imitation? Or to those others, philistines, worshippers of comfortable vulgarity: the self-appointed chosen representatives of God, the arbiters of the artistic life of a nation, the educators of the next generation? The merchants and traders in art, the parasites who patronize the true artists and gull the public; the putty-pushers of this world! Well, what can we expect but rejection from a public that is suspicious of all interference in its puritan culture. For a poet after all has no right to speak. No right.

'The baby cries. The children are hungry too: hungry bodies and minds and souls to feed, and they simple innocent creatures of God. And I haven't enough to provide well for them. To have children in our society is a penalty of the first order.'

A sudden hammering inside my head bangs for attention. Voices throbbing with malevolent glee. Could it be the voices of my parents, teachers, neighbours, relations, doctors, bank managers, psychiatrists, judges, policemen? The whole wearisome army of society, mobilized to enforce the cardinal reproduction of public opinion: "If he needs money, why doesn't he get a proper job?"

But how shall I defend you, when it is *she* who is living with you and Suffering for your Principles? It is *she* who is there to comfort you when you cry out in the night; *she* who sees your waking smiles, even if they are uninhabited as a ghost's. So let Duty defend you. Love, *in absentia,* cannot.

'A few hikers pass by in their branded clothes and heavy boots, startled and a little embarrassed to find people living in this ruin. They look up and hurry on, not to be contaminated. They hear no cry cradle reproof.

'Costly repairs must be done to the roof before winter sets in; and so I make a few shillings felling trees or cutting hay. My back aches, and my soul grows weary through unproductive labour. I have made for myself a strange prison of circumstance. Like an old man, slow and bent, I walk on the mountainside, away from the stench of cities and false gods. Today [forgive me, merciful spirits] I cursed and cursed.

'A rancour grows in me as always, and I eat out my heart. Perhaps I shall make strong poetry from this place. But anger consumes my life away. And you are not here to remind me how to smile. I play Beethoven to give me the will to continue.

'Oh, my dear, I hadn't intended to send you an inventory of my woes. Only to air these thoughts with you, to show you a mirror of my life, as it were... Tu comprends!

'And to write that you keep faith, a sanctuary within, a haven from which the bitterest blows can be faced. You will find the strength, my dear, as I have. Interruptions are always temporary if the will is constant.

'Night has fallen, and I shall try to sleep. When these words reach you, I shall have slept twice. And you, my dearest, in the centre of this night, are likely asleep, unaware that I make words to you. And find comfort in doing so.

'Our love is constant. To be apart is not to be strangers, but rather to meet in a different kind of time; a time in which all joinings are hallowed. *Then* to meet

is a true fulfilling of the spirit.
>'My love, my dearest one.
>'Richard.'

* * * * * * *

I walk through the morning to where the bracken bends across the edges of the horizon. Shame is seduced by an idle buzzard, sorrow defeated in the opening of marigolds. Heather spreads my path with affirmation like a royal carpet of assent.

Today I received a letter. It is the most beautiful thing that has happened to me in two weeks. It is the only thing that has happened to me in two weeks. It is my first love-letter. It breathes me. Memory encoded in every word… Nights mapped in the crevices of your skin. Your body painting my name. Your history embedding in my bones.

I walk across the fields, by boulders steadfast with the imprint of time. Before, their hard grey masks skulked at my contemplated demise; a chance messy intrusion upon these obelisks of immortality. Now they jab me, teasing, as I sit uncomfortably in that never-to-be-worn new dress, Compromise, and tell myself that I might, after all, have a place in the sun.

I have read your letter three times, once to the captive trees, once to the prickly silence sawing through the wilderness, and once to the lone cloud squatting like a mother hen over the possessive morning. I have read it, flushed with the whisper of your voice upon every word.

Your voice, rebirthing sound. Waking my soul from its hiding place in the corners of loneliness. Falling through dreams, landing inside the safe harbour of your arms.

But the more your letter sustains my love, the more it enshrines your absence. Three sheets of thin blue paper – what a pitiful substitute for a love that once rocked the world to sleep. And paper happiness is paper thin.

How static the world has become. How far away. I am drifting through the air on blue paper wings, with writing on one side. I'm growing smaller and smaller, fading away though the wrong end of a telescope. Soon I shall become an infinitesimal speck of dust, to be blown away with the cobwebs, or brushed off some gentleman's coat with disdain.

I have no pivot. Space is unpunctuated. I float like flotsam, tossed on these wild seas of longing. I have no gravity, except that of circumstance. And the grave, the only end.

I can no longer wrestle with the adversaries of God, and God is on vacation. There is only the desultory air; which has stopped breathing. And the world will go out with a whimper, not a bang.

Your absence annihilates me. I need you here to explain it to me.

* * * * * * *

Across this ragged wilderness, a jagged grey stone pushes through the undergrowth, half-way between the cottage and the hay fields. An in-between space. Sitting here, orphaned like A.A. Milne's little child, "I'm not really anywhere / I'm somewhere else instead.".

I bring pen and paper and thoughts and feelings and all my energy: a bowl of ingredients to make words. But the recipe eludes me. I haven't your talent, my darling. Words float on bird paths, are slippery as eels, uncatchable as soap bubbles.

I try to pluck words from the air, but they mutate from the joy of receiving your letters to the grief of your absence, before I can pin down their symbols on paper. Words, "the unhatched eggs of despair".

And if I have words, will your ears hear what my pen writes? [Language, too, has memory.] The word Love has a hundred interpretations. How can a few paltry marks scratched on a piece of paper excoriate what is in my heart?

So I send you only the poet's words, carved on my heart: "A pity beyond all telling / Is hid in the heart of love..."

Richard, hear my voice inside this small white envelope. Hear my voice.

* * * * * * *

Love has become a synonym for sickness of the soul. The summer sky broods with the insistent throb of space that is not you. The wind whinnies around invisible wounds. In the plaintive cry of a blackbird, my loneliness scratches.

I walk away to where the field turns the corner of my vision. Across the valley, impervious mountains rise like a heap of vicar's wives to keep me from my lover. A crow caterwauls to his mate, a cry relentless as the first call to arms. Clouds gather to gossip and thunder disapproval. The trees have shed their blandishments before their autumn leaves.

I am learning to live a new language, the language of loss. Words carved out of old ruins, devastation, jealousy. Slow words, sculpted from longing. The memory of your voice, hanging hair-thin on trees. The silence, grating with grief. Each moment not lived, moving me closer to death.

I cut my leg on a stone and watch the blood paint a viscid trail in the grass. I laugh with relief, the pain in my body anaesthetizing the pain in my heart. Momentarily. I didn't know I had so much blood left in me...

I watch birds rebuilding their continually violated nests. It gives me courage. It does not assuage my loneliness.

There is little comfort in talking to myself, or making love to myself; and there is no solace in the looking glass.

Late afternoon shadows my gloom. The willow weeps lamentations. Swallows pipe their mating-songs across the darkening sky with shameless unconcern for my sensibilities. The woodlice curl up for the night; even they are two. Only I sleep alone.

Is there nothing that can woo me with remembrance of joy, or bring back the hour of splendour in the grass?

* * * * * * *

I am loved. I have a love letter to prove it. I have read it, over and over. I know it by heart. In my heart. Carved into my heart. Bleeding...

Here nothing grows but weeds and self-deception...

* * * * * * *

Fear lurks in every corner of the cottage and my mind. Ghosts squeeze my heart, trespassing sun-scarred memories. I close my eyes against the thousand eyes of terror that pierce me through the lascivious darkness. The red of my blind eyes is all turned to blood.

Yet after all, "It is the eye of childhood that fears a painted devil... " And armed with this comforting lie, I grow courageous. I shall yet walk between the lines and squares of a London street, and say 'boo' to the waiting bears.

But not tonight. There's no moon.

Preparing for bed, I avoid too many precautions that could warn the chimeras of the night of the hugeness of my fear, and so invite their tricks. I dive suddenly beneath the bedclothes, in my nightdress of bravado. But not mosquito nets, nor barbed wire, nor stone walls that divide cities, can keep out the anguish that shadows me to bed.

My hand slips easily between my thighs, but brings neither comfort nor relief. I cannot beguile my body which knows your touch, your lips, your breath. The tortured rounds of my nipples weep the milk of stillborn love. Loneliness engorged, coursing through my veins.

"By night on my bed I sought him whom my soul loveth; I sought him but I found him not."

Oh, my bed is so cold without you.

"I opened to my beloved, but my beloved has withdrawn himself and is gone..."

Night-blind waste of life scurrying by in the unused darkness. The bedroom moaning with Dido's tears, as well as mine.

"I called to my beloved, but he gave me no answer."

Language of memory, graffiti of the mind.

"Without laughter... alone with remembrance and fear."

Silence is as final as death.

Have you forgotten
The dreams you sculpted
With my body
That night
You pierced
My inchoate flesh
Engendering in me
The aching joys
Of consummate
Aloneness...

Nine

Voices call our names in many languages: love, envy, curiosity, friendship, pity. Landscapes of the inner ear. Now, distant voices clamour inside my head, insistent as church bells in a hurry. A condescending cackle of advice for Life's Pilgrimage. How to Win Friends and Influence People – the outcast's almanac. Yes. I grew up on Little Women.

'You know Danielle, you're wallowing in a hell that only you have created.' Obviously; but don't we all create our own version of hell?

'What's all the fuss about? You're a good-looking girl. Find yourself another man – there are plenty more fish in the sea.' Yes, but I don't go so much for fish.

'As soon as you felt it happening you should have walked away.' But it happened before I knew... Before we met.

'What's all this love business anyway? It's family that counts, companionship, building a home together.'

No, my smiling tormentors, no! Benign mind doctors with malignant eyes, thin-lipped spinster school teachers of both sexes, or none, Spiritual Advisors, virginal community mothers – you've got it all wrong. Wearing your best Sunday habits of good advice to the young to mask your own regrets. The taste of shrivelled dreams on your lips, passions evicted by the wrinkles of compromise.

And what is the cost? What little cheatings, what fashionable deceptions have climbed you up your ladder of respectability? What grubby little lies, coughed behind polite cocktail-party fingers? Only occasionally, of course. But then increasingly, as you are not found out. And when did you last stop to smell a new flower in the hedgerow, or cry when a bird lay bleeding in the road; or make love, when you could have been busy making money?

Wearing Antigone's dress, I do not accept the meagre slice of cake you offer me in the name of happiness, provided that I promise to be a good little girl. I want the whole cake, unconditionally, and with cherries on the top. And if not, I don't want anything. For love is absolute, giving all or taking nothing.

Richard, Richard, which will it be? End my warring doubts. Be decisive, in my favour. Give me some sign of averment, or a way to be brave.

Oh little robin, gathering the resilient morning to cushion your love-nest, be on my side. Show me a way to endure.

I sit in the grass and wait for epiphany. I have exhausted every other possibility.

* * * * * * *

'Beloved,

'Your letters... thank you; one yesterday, two this morning. I read them several times, or rather, I heard your voice upon the words. The taste of your letter yesterday stays with me: simple, direct, real. An action had taken place in your heart and so you found the words necessary for sharing it.

'I believe that you will get beyond your feelings of self-pity, to reclaim that space where your soul may flourish and create. And then you will understand the true meaning of giving and receiving. For truly we need to give what we wish to receive. And whatever you feel you have received from me, know that I am but the instrument of its giving – the gift is not mine.

'You write that you want to "use time", rather than let time use you. And that you want to write. I take it you mean other than letters to me, though I hope it includes these too!

'If this is so, what's holding you back? Having, as you said, been "scribbling" since you were a child, you will know that the only way to "learn to write" is to write. And to read, of course. Read the great masters, again and again. They are the only education one needs – the great masters, in any art. You will have read the obvious English classics – Jane Austen, Dickens, the Brontes, George Eliot, Hardy. I would add to these Defoe, Stendhal, Tolstoy, Flaubert, Dostoyevsky, Svevo. This will give you the essential firm ground; it is the only way. And it is far better to read one good work ten times, than ten poor ones once.

'I would urge any aspiring writer to start with the classics precisely because they are further from us in form and style, and so offer a more objective study than those that are part of our immediate shared subconscious. Then, if you are stirred to, move on to more modern writers.

'Do not despair, dearest one. Do not. And do not think self-consciously of "finding your own voice". Write what you have to say. Then, if the work is honest and undertaken for its own sake – not for glamour, reward or success – your voice will emerge. You may find that you toil for months, or years. But one day you will wake up and realize that you have just found the right question. And then you can begin.

'I am not a novelist so I cannot say how this work comes about; I can only point out its necessary preconditions. And Canterbury, I believe, has several excellent libraries!

'Anna is now a little stronger, and takes the children off my hands part of the day. But it is hard for her too. She rages against this crippling domesticity; the continual demands of lively youngsters and of poverty wear her out. And she despairs, too, that she cannot return to her painting. She hasn't your faith, my dear. And faith is all. It is the clothing of the spirit.

'Now I turn to the questions you ask, and shall answer you with a poem:

"A Letter To One Who Asked:

"On the cliff, this hut,
which I built myself
under bank and brambles;
a single space and a hearth
fashioned from a ruin
on a remote difficult site.

The rock floor steps
from west to east;
that chimney embrasure
in summer traps light,
aligned to an October full moon
on the meridian, dates my work.
Wind and light from the sea...

You see this owl's bone?
When I first entered
his unravelled lodging,
weeds grew in the timbers,
the walls sweated mortar;

       bird-lime, dead mice, beetles.

       I troweled the sky out
       stencilled flame on the ground;
       and keep these fractured remnants
       whitened by wind and sun.

       On a hard day wind here
       whips salt into the skin
       and dries out the bones." **

'And so I work, and so drive out the anguish of your absence. For work, after all, is "love made visible". Perhaps I shall have completed this collection of poems by the end of the year. They form a fierce and valuable group, written in exile.

'But I doubt that this will bring much bread for the family. Our society loves nothing more than a tame poet that it can patronize. But one who dares to speak the truth? To question received moralities, to venture into the spirit, unarmed and unprotected by cloaks of fashionable sensibility. Now that's another matter!

'Art is bludgeoned at every crossroad under the deadening glare of city respectability. Pound's voluminous correspondence is a vitriolic attack from the same ground and on the same enemy. He reckoned that it takes eighty years for original work to reach the "general public"! No comment!

'And yet I warm to the work in hand. The quality of the struggle is after all its own reward. And I expect no recognition from a world that comforts itself with popular art. Verdi was not celebrated by the public until he was nearly forty, and had already written several great operas. Lampedusa's writing was not discovered until after his death. Cézanne was ferociously despised all his life.

'Well well. I am neither the first nor the only one to

curse our degenerate society that will not allow me to do the work for which I am fitted. That is, I shall do it; but who will pay the rent? This isn't a matter of sour grapes, the envy of all so-called failures for all so-called successes, but rather a need to set the record straight. I am sick to the soul of this Queendom "set in a silver sea"; and I am not alone. Schoenberg found the same in Vienna, and at seventy, the acknowledged father of modern music was writing begging letters in the States. And he was refused.

'Everything is done here by the backstairs, and truth is kept begging at the gate. And so the public, and particularly the artists, suffer. Oh my dear, I have such a catalogue of evils in my files, not because I have sought them out, but because I dared to notice them.

'But enough of this. I didn't mean to cry on your shoulder *in absentia*. These are thoughts of weakness, of my measure. To disclose myself to you, not to hide from you my moments of vulnerability; a weariness of spirit that gnaws at my heart. And my soul craves the solace that your smile would bring.

'But if I have put my anger into words, I have to that extent mastered it. And to whom shall I write these words, if *not* to you? Though I am powerless to change this iniquitous situation; and shall probably remain so. But the file is ready for when we open the case for the prosecution! Will you be there to hold my hand?

'I shall finish now, and go to pick wild mushrooms for our supper. We feed the little ones, who eat with healthy appetite, and lay them down to rest. We eat together, and talk of gentle things. Anna sleeps with the baby. I sleep apart, and dream of the dear one whose arms alone would comfort me. And pray that she is well, and finding strength in the struggle? I love you, and to watch the dawn break upon your lips is the only joy of a wearying old man.

'I think too often of the hours we spent loving in the hay. Summer has brought light rainfall, and today the fields are brushed with damp. But perhaps you would not mind too much?

'Dear heart, we shall find a way to be together soon. But first, like Napoleon on Elba, I must engineer my escape!

'Meanwhile, smiles and a gentle kiss,
'Richard.'

* * * * * * *

How tender the world is today. I walk across the fields to where the hay turns the edges of the world golden and curl up in my hidden place among the shrubs. The air is ripe with the smell of secret and forbidden things. Trees rise like temples of love to a refurbished God. Birdsong, caught on the breeze, circles me with endearments, like an unexpected halo. Even the lame sparrow has learnt to sing in tune.

Armed with paper and pencils, with dizzying ideas to deafen a draft of doubters, I sit in the soft grass and wait for a sign. Searching the arched sky, I see a gauntlet of huge letters painting itself across my horizon in soft clouds of purple and grey: 'WRITE'. I accept the challenge. This is not a choice, I realize, but a *need* bubbling up inside me, squirming to get out. A way of confronting my demons, I suppose; of framing the chaotic. Using artistic struggle as protection as well as metaphor.

And you have given me courage to begin to face the fear behind the fear. The fear of not being able to get past the words that camouflage vulnerability, to the simplicity beyond. The paralyzing fear not of writing, but of having to look into my own soul; of what I might discover, of what I might not discover. For the ingredients of any artistic endeavour must surely be the raw materials of the artist's life; to dissect, deconstruct, distil.

Daunting. Then I remember you telling me, one warm summer Sunday, not to 'think about being "a writer"; just be a woman who writes.' This is comforting. And something else you said: 'Don't be intimidated by labels and images that savage the purity of the creative impulse. Just get on with it; a workman setting out on a job.'

Writing; collecting an embryo of passions that are slowly beginning to stir inside me, that will come to term, I hope, in the 'tranquility of recollection'; 'breathing life into one moment, that wasn't there before'. Or is this just for poetry? The writer's struggle ultimately, I suppose, is to recognize the problems, to know they are unsolvable, but to keep wrestling anyway.

Deprived of theatre [I know, I know...] I find I am hungry for the struggle of creative endeavour; the grappling. And now I have got beyond the rubric of 'writer', I am flushed with words. Words filled with light, with morning sky, with possibility. Words, arching time. Language, remembering what memory forgets.

I shall paint for you an impressionist composition of my life here without you: the fastidious dance of the spider spinning its invitation to the fly that will be its lunch; the exact gradient of the grass-hoppers' hop; the stoop of the wind looking for itself in the trees.

I manage to fill six pages with existential trivia. Then, like a sudden cloudburst of torrential rain, your absence overwhelms me. Lost love, wailing in my womb.

And writing has made me hungry. I shall go in and prepare food. I don't want to crush the flame in defilement of the world…

* * * * * * *

God, come out of hiding in the branches of the old oak tree, and comfort me. I know you are there somewhere, because you keep disappearing. And I know that it is the believer who keeps looking for proof.

So, what shall be my plan for the next fifty years, if that is to be my sentence? To find God in the hedge at the bottom of the field? To reach the hedge at the bottom of the field?

Or not.

I walk through the dewy grass spiked with nasturtiums. A remote dirge wraps itself around the hills, in slopes of longing. A grey dusty day, not a day for making decisions. I shall send my thoughts out into the ether, to be collected at some future time. When the fog has lifted.

Now nature is out whoring, and rubs its fallacies into my private wounds. I clutch wildly at the nettles that provide the sting of salvation to the drowning, and wonder, what shall provide mine?

Time unwinds coils around my heart. There is nothing to do but wait, and try to decipher the code twisting through the mourning weeds its emblems of faith.

* * * * * * *

Hoarse grunts from the path leading up to the cottage interrupt my uninhabited morning routine. I run to greet this irregular visitor, more welcome here, or anywhere, than all others but one. But he deceives with unpredictable offerings.

'Dear Dani,

'Your very welcome letter was waiting for me when I got back from Manchester yesterday. I went up to meet some people who are keen to set up an International Socialist group there. We're trying to capitalize – if you'll forgive my use of such an obscene word! – our developing skills and not reinvent the wheel: organizing to share our experience [limited] and our resources [more limited!]. A really good bunch of people, but so few. But if commitment be the benchmark of success, then Macmillan and his comfortable cronies had better watch out!

'Dave came back from the Congo last week, and looks terrible. Months spent with haphazard food supplies, sporadic showers and hardly any mail. But a plentiful supply of dead bodies. What a story! The "noble rebels" fighting to rid their country of the evil Belgian Colonialists. And then turning on each other – factional fighting at its most brutal. But not battling as we characteristically do here on the Left, where anybody one finger to the right or left of you wants to set up a new faction because your ideology – in the light of today's new enlightenment – is no longer pure. And people that you were in bed with, so to speak, last week, now condemn you as a rabid subversive.

'But here we have the "luxury" of being able to indulge in such battles. Not so in the Congo. There, "political factions" are eating each other alive, not because of ideological differences but – over diamonds. Dave came back totally disillusioned. It's heartbreaking. And all of us, committed to political idealism, must learn to see and beware of naivety; or worse, its cousin gullibility.

'Now to your letter. Dani, I'm upset by what you wrote. Can you not get Richard sorted, one way or the other? The facts are the facts and you can't change them. But what you do about them is *your choice*. At the risk of sounding like your dearest friend who "never understands you", and for whom Great Emotion is – according to you – inexplicable, let me ask a couple of simple questions. Why are you still in the cottage if you're suffering so much? Why don't you come back to London? Or come up for a few days; I'll look after you, and promise to treat your feelings with gentle respect!

'And, of course, even "love" is culturally conditioned, and therefore political. In a different age, or a different country, you might have been one of several wives, or lived in a tribe where exclusive relationships were unknown. And I'm sure that the fledgling women's group, in which you were so active before you took off in a whirl for Canterbury, would have something to say on the subject!

'But more importantly, what's happened to the feisty iconoclastic Dani who was going to change the world? Does everything stop because you're "in love"? I think, on the contrary, love should be a spur to great things *in the world*. No?

'I'm glad you've gone back to writing. To paraphrase Bernard Shaw rather lamentably, I always thought of you as a writer whose "writing was interrupted by the theatre". I'd love to see something, when you're ready. And you don't have to impress *me!* Though if Richard is a *mench,* why would he be as critical as you fear? Doesn't this say something about him that you don't want to face? Or about your "image" of him? Or about your image of yourself, seen through his eyes?

'I see you already getting cross and twisting your hair round your fingers in that endearing nervous gesture of yours. Sorry if I've offended you. But I worry about you, Dani. And actually, I have to admit that I am curious about Richard. If he has managed to turn your life upside-down like this, he must be quite a guy.

'Beth and Alan send love. So do I. Please take care. And write soon!

'Love,

'Gerry.'

Dear Gerry. I am happy to receive his letter. But he believes that there is nothing in existence that does not have a political solution. How simple the world would be if this were true. And how diminished.

Gerry's letter breathes nostalgia through my bones, a recollection of forgotten innocence. That other life I lived, B.R., with Gerry and my friends in London; sharing long idealistic nights with Joan Baez and Pete Seeger, as we refined our strategies for changing the world. Banning all the evils that we could define: capitalism, the bomb, and government as we knew it.

Well, I have changed my reality, if not the world's. What paucity of achievement after such monumental struggle! From the faded ottoman, I look across at 'Pythagoras' table and see Richard sitting there, shaping words into a poem, looking up from time to time to mesmerize me with his grass-soft eyes. Now the cottage overflows with his absence. I make myself a mug of coffee, to buy myself time; to buy myself courage. To allow space for the gods to inspire me.

I look through the first tentative pages of my writing, endlessly revoiced, reworked, reformed. Redemption, of a sort. Here in the solitary silence of artistic endeavour, I may play God. For surely He is buried in the human heart; to give us divine perspective. And all creativity is only an attempt to earth Him, to give Him a human voice.

A writer, after all, may recarve time, challenging the laws of chronology, shaping sentient lives that never lived, reordering notes scribbled on the margins of dreams. Imagination, bursting the codes of the material world to bestow its own significance on the capricious patterns of human experience; a Lady Bountiful of Aesthetics. The only limitation, imagination itself; and a murderous lack of courage.

Life, on the other hand, remains chaotic, haphazard, forcing its own untidy adjustments willy-nilly. Perhaps it isn't the Great Tragedies that get us down in the end. It's the dirty sheets stuffed under the bed, ash all over the floor, the ubiquitous cloying stink of loneliness that no aerosol can dissipate.

Deceptions of a febrile world lying to ingratiate God.

* * * * * * *

Today I wrote a short story: 'They met. They loved. He left. The end.'

* * * * * * *

God has built his temple on the other side of the mountain and dragons breathing barbed impregnability keep mortal intruders away. How can I swim the moat of its fire, or scale the slippery walls armed only with arrows of desire? Anyway, it's too late. I am already washed up on the sands of the inevitable. I have struck the rock, in anger, in despair, and blood gushed forth. Now, like Moses, I shall never be allowed to reach the Promised Land.

Too many days alone in this leprous exile have built explosive facts, bumping into each other with fierce intent, establishing lies on the ground that no amount of gainsaying, afterwards, will undo.

I have no past. I was born, fully formed, the night you first wrapped me inside your thighs. Birthing love. Now I have only the cloak of your absence to clothe me.

Richard, I love you. But what does this signify in the face of this monstrous screeching bitch, The Facts? For you are with *her*, you are not with me. You are not with me *because* you are with *her*. And armed with all the rosy weapons of love, I can do nothing to change what is.

My body, broken with welts of longing, shudders in the night.

Why do you come to me
No more
You
Who took from me
The laughter
Of my girlhood dreams
Unblemished
And sired
The carnal non-dream
Of my womanhood…

Ten

Stone dust, muted sounds, stillness. The wind weaving gentle stories among the brambles. The canopy of the earth spreading affirmation.

Through the long balmy summer, I am bombarded with words from across the Welsh border. New words. Other words. Words of life and love, of daring and delight. Words tumbling into my eyes, tangling with each other, dancing through my mind like quicksilver.

My grumpy hunchback visitor wearily tramples the bracken to my door. He is overworked; he has visited me every day this week, bearing offerings in assorted re-used envelopes. Fragments of love, parts of the whole. The whole. Truant words, fleeing the page, entering my heart. Breathing my heart...

He grumbles, having to trudge up the hill so often on his old rusty bike, his old rusty legs. Suddenly, it strikes me that he might withhold letters till several had accumulated, to make the journey worthwhile in his eyes. It freezes me with horror, then galvanizes me into action.

I invite him in for a cup of tea. He accepts as though

he's doing me a favour. Perhaps he is. He looks around the cottage in disbelief, as if he had entered a space warp. He takes in the dust on the furniture, the dirty plates in the sink, the reek of loneliness stifling the air. Then he settles onto the ottoman as though it had always been his place.

'You here on your own, then?'

'Yes.'

He looks at the letters he's just handed me, at my sadness, and softens.

'Boyfriend?'

His definition, not mine. But I nod, anyway. He stares at me, as though trying to make a connection – so many letters, but why isn't he here? Why indeed! He grimaces, the nearest his large bearded face comes to a smile. I offer him biscuits.

A long silence. He dips a biscuit into his tea, then loses it in crumbs in his spreading beard. He makes strange sucking noises, while his eyes roam the walls, finding nothing on which to settle. Finally, he clears his throat twice and, sure of my attention, speaks:

'I loved a woman once. When I was young – and handsome.' He laughs. 'A real looker she was, I can tell you. Here.' And out of his worn saddlebag, he takes an old sepia photograph of a beautiful young woman, yellowing round the edges.

I am moved beyond words that this crusty old man should still carry around with him his sweetheart's photograph. I look at him as though for the first time; I see not a hunchback, not a postman, but a human being.

'What happened to her?'

He sits in unreadable silence for so long that I feel I've intruded into some dark private place where no-one is welcome. Finally he says, 'She married my brother. They've got four kids. All grown now.'

I pour him more tea. He adds sugar absentmindedly,

three or four spoons, and stirs; and stirs. Then, suddenly breaking the silence, he talks in short sharp bursts, spitting out words like machine-gun fire. He tells me that he lives a few miles up the road, in the old stone house where he was born before the First World War. His people have been farmers for generations. When his parents died, his brother took over the farm, but he stayed on in the house. And he lives as his family has done for hundreds of years, inhabiting the seasons, in touch with a simple God. Reading a few oil-lit verses from the Bible every night.

'I like to read. Books,' he adds, to make sure I've understood. 'I travel round the world. Not in boats, in books!' He makes a strange sound, somewhere between a grunt and a laugh. He gulps down the rest of his tea, looks at the plate of biscuits, weighs up his options, takes another one, and leaves.

Now whenever he has post for me, he comes in for a cup of tea. His visits are thrice blessed. He brings me love and affirmation from beyond the Welsh hills. He tells me stories of the local people, legends to make your blood curdle, handed down through the generations to children sitting by open fires on the laps of their soft-voiced, black-shawled mothers. And he brings me books.

One at a time, he brings me old leather-bound classics, the pages yellowed with reading: Dickens, Jane Austen, Thomas Hardy. He insists that I borrow them – and read them, so we can discuss them later. For his real purpose is to fill empty hours, sharing his love of people who live in books. It's easier than loving people who live in the world. That's the unspoken deal: his books and conversation for my tea and time; his lonely pride for my unproud loneliness. *Quid pro quo.*

And so, serendipitously pincered between the guidance of my lover and the gifts of my postman, I resign myself to resuming my literary education. What God has decreed joined, let no man put asunder!

It was the worst of times; perhaps it was becoming the best of times...

* * * * * * *

Down the Welsh mountains, bundles of words come galloping towards me; mysteries unravelling, wild visions caught on the wing and tamed, washed up with summer showers on the near shore of love.

'... Your letters, thank you. Dearest heart, your words cheer me indeed; they are the clothing of the spirit. I, too, am passing through a kind of otherwise time. This morning, I walked by the cliffs and watched the sea, waves six foot high crashing their fishy tales along the coast. The air was cool and cleared out the cobwebs. I met a careful beetle on its walk across the sand and saw a jellyfish washed up with its own story to tell.

'Last night I played the Beethoven quartet – the last Razumovsky. And I saw you sitting on our bed in my nightshirt, the outline of your breasts shimmering with the music. And the rapt expression on your face as the quartet embraced you that, even as I recall it, makes my heart quiver. And my memory stroked your hair, your glorious black silk hair falling over your breasts. And I felt able again to see summer in winter things.

'I look forward to many more nights of Beethoven with you. Many more nights...'

Sheets of words, echoing on the wind; invisible connections, stronger than silence. Orbits of words spinning towards me, harvesting sunlight, embracing my heart. Love falling down the hillside into my lap.

"Let him kiss me with the kisses of his mouth; for thy love is better than wine."

And I am all mouth like a new-hatched bird, open

only to this one pervading hunger, waiting to be filled with the food of love.

Belief, like medicinal herbs, may take centuries to cultivate, but I am reaping now the ripe fruit of all earth's offerings. I am the seed and the flower. I am the womb.

* * * * * * *

Today Thomas, my faithful postman, arrives later than usual. He hands me three letters. I am hungry, so I make him a sandwich. He eats and watches me, making invisible connections, it seems, between me and the cottage.

After the silent ritual stirring of his sugared tea, he asks: 'Why did he leave?'

'Sorry?'

'The boyfriend. Why did he leave?'

Why did he leave? What words can I find to answer him? To answer myself. He left because duty overwhelmed desire. He left because his faith in our interlocked dreams was subsumed by responsibility to four small cries of need. To a fifth cry. Louder. Menacing.

'He has a wife' I said.

Thomas leaves slowly, leaving something of himself behind.

I take the letters with the South Wales postmark. But one looks different. Is this the writing on the wall?

'Dear Danielle,

'By chance I came upon one of your letters to Richard, and decided to write to you. Forgive me for having read it. This was not prompted by vain curiosity; you are important to Richard, and so at least vicariously to me.

'Richard and I are irrevocably intertwined. I also

married his aspirations, and have loved him and suffered with him for ten years, all that a woman can love and suffer for a man. And it hasn't been easy. There are times when I think it an extraordinary indulgence that he should devote his time to writing, when the children cry from cold or hunger. And I cannot allow myself even to think of buying a tube of paint.

'And yet I know that we are a part of each other; even in our conflicts we live through each other. A strange symbiosis.

'But Richard needs you too. You are young and fresh and I'm sure there is much you can give him. And I am weary...

'So, here I am, and there you are, and there is Richard, somewhere between, and somewhere beyond in a world of his own. And maybe we'll get together some day.

'What am I really trying to say? Maybe just "hello".

'Yours,
     'Anna.'

Anna... She has read my letters? One? Two? All of them? The ones with the jungles and the juices and the jealousy? The passions and the pity, the rage and the rancour? The desperate naked longing...

Down in the knife-sharp grass, among the sawing of the grasshoppers, I scream mortification in the wind. How can she move with such appalling confidence among the poor, dispensing cakes of beneficence like a latter-day Marie-Antoinette? Is she not also afraid of the guillotine?

I gather up a crumpled ball of paper. It sizzles in my hand, burning all curiosity. I crush it between fingers shaking with rage. I laugh indifference at its presumption. How can a cheeky scrap of paper hurt me?

But I burn it anyway; in a rusty tin can in a fetid corner of the wilderness. A fitting end to *her* impertinence. A pyre of wasted words. Cinder on the rubble of history.

But you cannot burn knowledge; burn words to eradicate ideas. It never works; it re-ignites lost power. A phoenix of faith rising from the ashes; wisdom of burnt books rekindled sevenfold, down the generations.

I strain my eyes across the hills to conjure Richard's face. But *her* image emerges, slowly, like a negative photograph in developing spirit. Definitely negative. Unreadable eyes, and lips freshly painted with my lover's kisses. I do not know her face, but recognize the unfurling triumph of her smile. She wears the knowing glance of an angel that cuts the summer sky in two.

I no longer understand the rules: behaviour that wears no uniform, words that pronounce a new sentence on my life. How dare she presume to understand, or woo me by mischievous cleverness into thinking her disguise to be charitable? Get thee behind me, Anna!

So I had named her; to myself I had named her, this *Other,* this dark *She,* who trespasses my life with oppressive ubiquity, wounding me daily, and oh most especially nightly. *She* has given me a one-way ticket to the cave of Trophonius, and will yet bless my journey.

Damn you, Anna. Damn you. Why did you have to force your existence on me? No, I will not be bought by your treacherous gestures of magnanimity. A thorn by any other name... So pave your pathway to sainthood with another's tears. And keep your noble smiles of complicity to yourself.

* * * * * * *

One summer, when we were children, we were taken to the seaside for the holidays. And I stood for hours with one foot in Brighton and one foot in Hove, fascinated that I could be in two places at the same time. But the world has grown up since then. And now I see you, with one arm across Anna's shoulders, the other reaching out towards me. Your eyes are tortured, and I cry for your suffering also. You wear a schizophrenic mask – half love, half pity. But I am no longer sure which face is turned towards Anna, and which towards me.

* * * * * * *

But then new pieces of love arrive, tumbling out of scruffy brown envelopes. Torn from your heart:

'Beloved... No end, no beginning. Only the Word, indivisible by time. And you, bathed in an aura of light, in the centre of this night. Loneliness wraps itself around my heart, and I crave the solace of your smile; falling into your dreams, holding the night inside you...'

I retrace the language of love: getting lost together, finding each other, finding ourselves. Wild nights burning in your eyes, wearing you like roses through clothed days, your smell inside my skin. The breath of love...

'I pause for a few moments in the work needed to keep a roof over our heads, and play a little music to restore my sanity. And take pleasure in talking to you...

'Family relations have not been without acerbations, but are calmer now. Yet always the desperate gnaw of poverty like a plague of rats inside my skull; which is after all my responsibility. It is a kind of escape to sit here and write: to make poetry, but that is my work; to make words to you, but that is my love...

'And remember, dearest one, for my sake, I am not absent from you if I am present in your heart.'

Present in my heart, yes. In my dreams, my memories, my meditations. But not in my bed.

'Your last letter brought me great delight; the delight of a man reimbursed a hundred-fold by the words of his lover. And also joy that you are finding the strength to reach that stillness inside you, your own centre. For one has to keep a sanctuary within, a dwelling place from which the bitterest blows may be faced. I found that I could not discover this for myself in the city. And then one must translate the exodus, from flight into necessary creation. For even into the desert we take a mirror... '

The mirror that I hold in my desert faces westward. It reflects the gift of sunlight, poetry holding up the night sky, your eyes laughing... And now my mirror also smiles on me: this is the face that lured the archangel into my bed; the face that launched rivers of nights, flowing with belonging.

My tears, that once cried a moat around the world, have become waterfalls of unbearable gratitude.

'I am weary from a long day's toil, but my bed no longer brings comfort. I stretch out my hand, but it is empty. Oh that you were here to embrace my soul...

'I try to sleep – a backlog of fatigue to dispose of. But your elongated absence holds me awake. I think of that peace that we shared, afterwards... That blessed sea of peace.

'Dearest heart, this letter is its own seal.'

* * * * * * *

I go out into the fields behind the cottage. My body, without direction from me, begins to move; breath of love, moving my limbs, my head, my hips; my heart. I start to dance, my body lusting with life. The rhythms of this new joy pulsate through my veins, as I twirl and twist and whirl and leap. My limbs move of their own volition, arms and legs and hands and feet reaching outwards into the universe, touching the earth, touching the sky. I dance, an ecstasy of love made visible; and all of nature dances with me. I am floating, weightless, my body pure motion, a dervish of delirious delight. The music of the spheres fills me, crescendos. I fly, my body merging with the wind, my arms wings that carry me above the clouds, higher, higher...

Breathless, my body reborn in movement, I float back to earth, landing gently on the welcoming softness of grass. I sit on the earth, a woman alone in a field of bluebells. Not alone...

* * * * * * *

In his last letter, Richard wrote 'I love you' in eleven languages. In one.

* * * * * * *

I walk across the wilderness towards the hay fields beyond, to revisit the sighs of a summer night... But my foot slips on a rusty tin can of mouldering paper cinders, and memory reverses itself. Anna, my gentle tormentor, it's time to save your intrusive smiles to balm your future wounds. For the interim, mine and yours, is nearly over.

And if the path to my deliverance lies over your mangled hopes and dreams, I shall walk it with firm steps, and dark glasses to shield my eyes from the bloodied trail behind. And I shall leave Pity in my wake, dressed in her virgin mourning robes, to bathe your wounds, to cry rivers of mercy for your grieving empty breasts.

Over your sorrow I shall spread my wedding sheets. And compassion will remember you nightly in my prayers.

I have waited for you
Empty
As the wastes of the moon
Hanging desolation
On the hooded night
I have grown old
In waiting for you
In space
Absent from myself
In time before
Tears
Were born...

Eleven

Time, scurrying down the centuries, is a blind prophet. It creates an invisible present, a slow-burning narrative wandering through space, looking for itself in the dark. Yesterday, today was tomorrow. Tomorrow, today will be yesterday. Time coils in circular riddles, deceiving with relativity. And single-handed, time keeps me from my lover.

But without time, how should we know when to eat, when to sleep, when to think? "Vanity, vanity, all is vanity..." Yes yes, all things in their appointed season: a time to plant and a time to reap; a time to weep and a time to laugh; a time to mourn and a time to dance. Only tell me, when will the hour of love come round again?

My watch is broken, and I have no money to repair it; no reason. So how will you rule me now, Time, without your ministering angel to mark the hours and seconds upon my wrist? But we deceive ourselves with time, the great illusion of the human mind. We carve it in prescribed parcels of space, through our own nervous need to feign control. So we rob eternity to nail the coffins of our insecurity.

I wander in the heather, abstracted. I do not know which day is which. And unlike Esther in ancient Persia, I haven't seven dresses with which to name the seven days of the week. I devise new ways to kill time. But time refuses to die.

I do not know any more whether I am old or young, or which season will wake me tomorrow.

* * * * * * *

Your absence aches in me like a phantom limb. It seeps into every crack and cranny of the cottage, cloistering loss. And the cottage hides its memories in shame. My dreams peel off the walls like rotting wallpaper. No signs of the passion that once painted these pasty rooms with pagan hymns to Eros and Aphrodite. All that remains is the warp of love, encrusted in stone.

Then, I was reborn every night in your arms. Now loneliness cries me to sleep; and wakes me, throbbing inside my scalp. For more than a week, no letter from you.

On the faded ottoman I sit and stare, eyes full of cataracts, scouring the cottage for its buried heart. I look at my painted Polish fisherman, bought in another life, it seems, when a twenty-year-old woman, ripe with love, moved with her lover into an ageing cottage. The first original painting I ever bought. It will take me a year to pay for it, one pound a week. But when I'm hungry, it sustains me.

I know he's a fisherman because he has a fish on his head.

I light a cigarette. I have nothing else to do. The ill-fitting windows rattle the edges off my nerves. The gash in the roof slashes the cottage open to the skies, but allows no sunlight to disturb my present gloom.

The prison bars inside my head lattice my despair.

The fisherman stares back at me, probing, demanding answers. He remembers my nakedness. I cower in his gaze, and go outside. But I am drenched in memories of you held between the cottage walls; each time I go out, a little less of me emerges.

The stream washes the world with a muddy trail of sorrow, and nobody walks on water anymore. Stones stagger under the weight of time; the sky broods ashen grey, the empty wind offers no foothold. When did William Blake become my fallen god?

I hear the distant beat of drums in the trembling of the earth. Rain clouds blister with menace. Birds screech, terrorizing the air, accountable to no-one. Slugs gorge soundlessly, waking demons in the grass. Loneliness is carnivorous. It is eating me up, and will leave nothing for the worms. Only time remains, the thief of truth.

Sirens from distant ships hoot inside my head, cargoes from remote and forgotten ports carrying your absence.

Was so much blood spilled just to make me a philosopher?

Yes, yes. And eternity is only a word.

* * * * * * *

In my single bed at night, loneliness has me splayed on the rack. The screams of the world's tortured quail in my belly. I writhe, I contort myself through agonies of lust. I am mangled, utterly, in my sex.

Dear God, I cannot stand the pain any longer. I cannot. I shall go out into the night, and take the first man I find. Again. And again. To feel the weight, the hard male weight of a man's body pushing down on mine, the relentless thrusting throbbing thrashing into my open wound. Two bodies grappling against each other, reaching in the darkness the nowhere of their existence.

Richard, forgive me these faithless thoughts, but understand what your absence is doing to me. Tonight I will not love you tenderly, not even in my dreams; or yours. For the storms of this poisonous celibacy raging across my famished flesh will not abate. Tonight I can only scream out one potent consuming four-letter word. And it is not love.

****

I am losing count. I have not bled for several weeks; it must be six, or maybe seven. I accept this as an arbitrary fact of my existence here, in exile from the world, signifying nothing. Then it strikes me as an ill omen from the nether gods. I have sinned in love and now am punished: I have ceased to be a woman.

But time again proves its capricious power, and forces upon me another realization: I am become too much a woman. My belly is swelling with the seeds of love...

Flesh of my flesh, blood of my blood. And yours. Writing a new biography with my body; too deep for words.

I go outside. I sit on the steps of the veranda, moved by incantations of sky, caught between weathered rocks. I stare up at the moon, spilling over the edge of the night, ebbing into prophecies: at feather brush of butterfly wings; at the Picasso shapes of wild wolves caught in the shadows. I howl, and the wolves howl with me. Calling the ancestors, connecting to my power. Woman power; a chain of women pushing through the birth canal of history, reaching out to this embryonic new life...

But what shall I tell you, my little one, when the future arrives and you will ask me those questions that no amount of dissembling can answer?

'Does my daddy love me?'

'Yes, my darling, he loves you.'

'Then why isn't he here?'

I try to decode the messages that time is carving with my body. I contemplate the weight of clouds, looking for signs. Thin knuckles of sun begin to crack open the morning, drizzle a haze of possibility through clotted air. Today it is Sunday, for I hear church bells in the distance calling the would-be faithful to prayers. But unlike St Joan, the voices that I hear in their ringing are not of God.

So I live in otherwise time, suspended across the latitude of silent sorrow, grave and impotent as a royal eunuch.

Now it is no longer Sunday. It is Munday. Wet with future tears, I throw myself back into the indifferent tasks of physical survival, welcoming them, as a priest may welcome the trivia of his vocation, not to have time to think about God.

* * * * * * *

Time is out of joint. Or I am.

The air turns suddenly cold, reminding my frailties of mortality. The staccato pains of late summer have given birth to the autumnal air. The gathering clouds are rolling pastry on the roof. The wind is desolate.

A hard grey time, the crabby air warning birds to prepare for long journeys. The new face of the old world. But whichever mask she wears, I am tired of her grumpy imputations. Each day is a renewed struggle, to keep the seepage constant.

I shall go to collect firewood, and slowly build the

pyre of my immolation.

* * * * * * *

Thomas cranks his bicycle across the undergrowth and I run to greet him; his first visit for ten days. I rush our tea ritual, anxious for him to be gone, impatient to read the missive that he brings.

'Danielle dearest,

'Your last letters disturbed me. You are not made to be solitary, and maybe it is harming you. Nor is it necessary, though it may be necessary in order for you to learn this. So, shall I say to you, "Forsake the path you have chosen; go back to London, to your family, your friends?" To do this is not to have failed.

'If you are determined upon your present solitude, then know why you suffer, and understand the struggle. Only then will you find the necessary strength to endure. For we cannot know what we are in an afternoon, nor on a twentieth birthday. Nor, in the very truth of it, can we know what we are without dying that most harrowing of all living deaths...

'And so we pass through the pains of the flesh, and these pains we confuse with suffering. Now to suffer is to allow ["Suffer the little children to come unto me..."] To know that one suffers, and to *consent* in that suffering, most especially against the strongest of our desires. And that the agents of it are but agents. For what we want, is not what we desire, but what we lack. ["The Lord is my shepherd, I shall not *want*..."]

'Only then can one truly die, and be reborn. If, as you write, you have died many times – '

I have died every night that has closed my eyes in darkness that doesn't embrace you.

' – then you have not yet died at all. Desire is not of the flesh but of the mind. Don't be misled by what is known only to shallow minds and popular concepts. For the Eternal is immutable – and "not a sparrow falls but Heaven knows it".

'You are tender of soul, my dear, and seeking "in the spirit". Do not be ground down by images you have of your suffering. Just allow...

'For me now, work is all. Which accounts for much of my anger, and not a little of my invective; obstacles which are the result of stupidity, which prevent work. Michelangelo said, "A man paints with his brains not his hands, and therefore I can do nothing until I am allowed justice." But I cannot wait for justice. Happily, the stink here is of poverty, not of corruption; the air outside is fresh. Only inside there is a heaviness. Ah, Danielle...

'But work drives out despair, and one accepts the toil, without sight of the end. And in one sense, outside impositions make greater achievement possible. Though the source of all restriction is within the artist himself.

'Look at the lives of any great writer, painter, composer. What they all have in common is a personal sense of inadequacy in their own work, which is constant. For the true artist has always failed in that which he has not done; and there is always that which he has not done. And in a way, it is this sense of failure that drives the work forward; it is the very ground of achievement.

'Our society, of course, does not help. People with a "good education" somehow feel *entitled* to "Art". It's part of their social equipment! But this puritanical culture's concept of art is one that endorses its own morality and patriotism, seeking not to enhance its aspirations, but to corroborate its prejudices. And what is morality if it is only the trappings of good behaviour?

'As Yeats says in *The Choice:* "The intellect of man

is forced to choose / Perfection of the life, or of the work, / And if it take the second, must refuse / A heavenly mansion, raging in the dark."

'I am sending you a few lines of a poem I'm working on. The only present I can give you at the moment. As yet it's untitled, but is written to The State:

> 'I saw an old man of wisdom, peace,
> prepare for death, more fit to live than many;
> the poet who walks in broken shoes,
> begs an old shirt, a corner, ease.
> Dressed in scarlet fungus the State stands
> ready, like the footman at a party
> for a week-end chat; the cunning usurer
> in his glass mansion hides out of sight;
> all men's blood seeps through his hands. **

'And so I shall leave this page, which I send to you with my blessings; and return to the work in hand. You will overcome present afflictions, my dear; in them we fashion our soul. And again I say keep faith, for this is a touchstone, a fulcrum of sanity.

'We put out our hand in the dark to make sure that the landmark has not moved; it has not.
    'As ever,
       'Richard.'

****

The bruise of your letter stains the cottage. I go outside. I crush the pages with icy fingers, but Judas' epistle burns my hand. 'The air outside is fresh.' Indeed.

Thomas is sitting on the bottom step of the veranda, looking out across the fields. As though he were waiting for me. As though he knew. I sit on the steps, away from him, orphaned in my pain, wrapped in the sour smell of your words.

Somehow, Thomas' presence insinuates itself; a blind man whose touch you cannot refuse. And the measured way he draws on his pipe, reminiscent of… This is one image too far for me, the one that breaks the camel's back. And I burst into a caterwauling of sobs, on and on, unleashing my pain, my anger, the crippling rawness of my soul. Between wails that could raise the dead, I wrench out my heart:

'I can't reach him – he's married to his poetry – he says I have to die – why isn't he here? – his wife reads my letters – when will he come back to me? – "not a sparrow falls but heaven knows" – I'm pregnant, for God's sake, pregnant – did you know that Michelangelo painted with justice? – our love was sacred – all great artists are failures – suffer the little children – I KNOW why I am suffering – who the fuck cares about Michelangelo? – why has he betrayed our love? – I'm carrying his child and he preaches to me about Art – why isn't he here? – I don't want his poetry, I want HIM – I can't live without him – I can't, I can't …'

Exhaustion dries my sobs. The punctured air resumes its voiceless vigil. In the solemn silence, wet with my tears, Thomas grunts, reaches out a tentative hand towards me, then withdraws it with touching humility. I wipe my eyes on my sleeve, withering in embarrassment.

And so we sit, in a long separate silence. After uncountable minutes, out of the depths, Thomas says: "'The Lord giveth and the Lord taketh away.'" And he sighs.

* * * * * * *

How sterile knowledge has become. It devastates my mind with insignificance. That "instant arrested in eternity" has slipped off the pages of your letter, and crouches in shame. Dear God, where in all this brilliant subterfuge of language is there an echo of the Word that Was in the Beginning?

Love is usurped. The round keys of your typewriter need blush no longer. So, bang out fierce words upon that faithless machine. Proselytize the philistine. Buy your coveted place in literature. Will this acquit you of my murder?

Once, you carved poetry upon my lips; stole through the night to consummate our love with Milton's dream. Once in that sea of nights, you "mounted the Trojan walls / And sighed [your] soul towards the Grecian tents / Where Cressida lay..." Once, your body was the instrument that penned all metaphor.

Once the Muses were not my enemy.

Wasn't it you who said that you felt alone on earth when I laughed and you didn't know why? That the world had turned cold when I spoke a name you did not recognize? And now you write to me of suffering, of dying? Of Art? Art parcelled between leaves of love. What blasphemy of belief your words interpret. But more lacerating than all the ugly words you write to me, are the words you do not write.

I am confused. Language has shed all meaning, or writes philosophy's texts to hide hypocrisy. I am stuck up on the Tower of Babel, terrified of the bricks raining down on me. I am struck dumb with language. And you tell me that we each compile our own dictionary of destruction!

The landmark *has* moved. And behind your treacherous words, another voice insinuates itself across the lowing of my grief: 'Here I am, and there you are, and there is Richard, somewhere between, and somewhere beyond in a world of his own.'

Anna, move over on your cold hard bench of inevitability, and make room for me.

* * * * * * *

It's five o'clock in the morning. I am oppressed by tiredness, but my faithful insomnia keeps watch over the night. I cry, far away. My soul, far away. Your smell on my pillow has evaporated.

Once, I had a lover. But now my soul wears a body you would not recognize, and shame hides my nakedness from the prying eyes of the dark. My passions are belied by this gnarled old trunk. My breasts hang shrivelled as rotten pears and the gash between my legs is dried up and my body sags beneath the weight of dead dreams and the relentless gnawing of this untouched flesh.

Why do you come to me no more, my love, my heart?

I have waited for you, through the long balmy days of summer turned to dust.

I have waited, across crusted hours of space worn thin by cankerous rats; searching barren planes of time's horizon.

I have waited till now.

And Now consumes me.

Shall I never sleep quietly, and wake to a new tomorrow?

Shreds of remembrance
Dying fragments
Of dreams
Bandaging the wounds
Of remorse
Memories
Locked
In the worm's head...

Twelve

"But the best laid plans of mice and men..." Thomas, my faithful postman, now bloated with power, though unbeknown to him, pulls out of his worn saddlebag another possibility.

'My darling child,
    'More than two months have passed since we were together, and my soul grows weary in your absence. I love you, and your suffering drives daggers through my own loneliness.
    'Anna is not too well, and I cannot see my way to leaving her at the moment, with all the demands of the family. But I am impatient to be with you – even work is no longer a palliative for your absence. And work I must, but your image constantly disturbs me.
    'Dear heart, will you not find a way to visit us? Anna would like to meet you, and I should treasure you for as long as you would stya. [You see, my fingers are fatigued, and I strike the wrong keys; I need you near me to remind me of the time when I was young!]
    'Dearest one, come to me, for I cannot now come to you.

'My love, my heart.
'Richard.'

* * * * * * *

YES!! But no… How can I go? But how can I not go? I sit in this reinvented Eden and pick petals off a dandelion. I shall go. I shall not go. Yes. No. Yes. No. Yes. No. One petal is left, but divides into two at its tip: yes and no...

* * * * * * *

Today the world is restored to its proper orbit, and all of nature is reborn with me. Oh gentle blackbird, sing out your song to mark this hour, which is all hours; and little robin, red and pious, hopping among the shrubs without influence, weep no longer. For this moment is what all moments have been waiting for, why time has cheated me; and why the vines of faith, like liberty, take so long to grow.

Suddenly I am ashamed of the lethargy lying at my feet. I shall launder the dirty sheets strewn across the floor, wash the pile of dirty dishes weighing down the sink, sweep the ash off every covered surface. I shall cut the sprawling weeds of my self-pity.

Yes, Richard, yes. Of course I shall come. Though to comply is surely to embrace madness. But I have waited too long. Now the miracle hangs ripe to burst the space between us, spreading the future hour across the sky, waiting to be inhabited...

But of course I cannot go. For whom should I be as I entered your home, Anna's home, in her eyes? Or in mine. She will hold up a proprietary mirror to the green fantasies we have woven with the tangled threads of each other's souls. And I fear bloody murders in her castle if I grant her the role of "honoured hostess".

But every fibre in my body quivers towards the Welsh Mountains, and longing fills the footsteps where grief replaced love. My heart sings. I shall listen and go.

But my head has other ideas and rules me with iron reason. I stand back. I inhabit pretended objectivity. I weigh the pros and cons but the scales heave in a frenzy of indecision. I wrestle with my conscience. And then a sudden moment of epiphany. I shall go if Anna invites me. And armed with this delicious impossibility, I paint fantasies of journeys, down in the rustling grass.

Inside the envelope is another sheet of paper:

'I send you this poem, which is from Edwin Muir's "Collection"; a volume I should like to give you, but I am poor!

"Circle and Square

"I give you half of me;
No more lest I should make
A ground for perjury.
For your sake, for my sake,
Half will you take?

Half I'll not take nor give,
For he who gives, gives all.
By halves you cannot live;
Then let the barrier fall,
In one circle have all.

A wise and ancient scorner
Said to me once: beware
The road that has no corner
Where you can linger and stare.
Choose the square.

And let the circle run
Its dull and fevered race.
You, my dear, are one;

Show your soul in your face;
Maintain your place.

Give, but have something to give.
No man can want you all.
Live and learn to live.
When all the barriers fall
You are nothing at all."

* * * * * * *

I walk across the fields to where the hay turns the edges of the world golden and come face to face with my incipient future. She is clad in summer smiles, and greets my disbelief with infectious laughter. The gentle breeze brushes confirmation through my hair, and mother earth embraces me, welcoming me among her daughters...

"Come, oh thou fairest among women, for thou art as a garden of sweet fruits, as a fountain of living waters; lie down with us, for also our bed is green."

And I lie down in the long grass, swollen with this marvellous new disease. I am the fertile ground of all metaphor, transformed by love's potency.

And more. For I am pinned to that centre of all worlds, blessed with that love whose consequence is the skipping approach of the next generation. And I float away on the watery fusions of love, with the fledgling advent of these inside seas of joy as my sail. Oh the fruits of love, the gentle suffusing fruits of love!

He has set his seal upon our love. And I am all of nature, lush with fecund miracles, shaping the earth in my image, ready to birth a new world.

Warm air scatters skirts of dewdrops, undressing sentiment. Hot fingers of sun touch memory into meaning.

Now is the winter of our discontent indeed made

glorious summer.

****

Dusk: a faint-hearted moon chases the sun home; birds, flying south, pin down the darkening hour. I sit in the cottage, wrapped in the silence of evening shadows, in promise.

In the cracked looking-glass, I examine my swelling breasts, the dark protrusions of my nipples straining jauntily towards their future role. I smile with the pride that is also swelling my belly. Richard, why aren't you here to witness the metamorphosis of your love?

Suddenly, I am afraid: this condition that, like plane crashes and B.O., only happens to other people, has finally caught up with me. A year ago I was a starry-eyed virgin, on my way to becoming a Great Actress. Now, I'm in love with a married man, the father of four children; expecting his child. 'Dear Evelyn Home... ' Dear dear.

Forgive me, God, but no washer-women philosophers will succeed in causing me even one grain of guilt. Sadness, yes. Grief. But not for my swelling belly, only for the absence of its cause.

Oh my baby, push through the curtain of pain, acquit us all of past murders with your birth. Answer the happy accident of biology with undefiled smiles. My child, my embryonic truth, swim through the blood, be my salvation, as well as your own.

But no, no. This is your hour, and you, my darling, must rise up and mark it as your own. For if you are to be my salvation, and your child yours, when shall be born the one who will claim her own prize with her own blood?

Oh, brave new world...

****

Today Thomas excels himself and brings me three letters. One from Beth, asking when I'm coming back to London. One from Gerry, not exactly asking:

'Dear Dani,

'Thanks for your letter. I read with interest what you say about writing. I am certainly not a novelist, but maybe the process is not too far removed from journalism? The same driving force to uncover truth – fact or fiction – to stand up and make a statement.

'Anyway, my advice – not that you've asked for it, of course – would be that if you are serious about writing, then just get on with it. Forget your fashionable image of the "suffering artist". Don't keep taking your emotional temperature to see if you're 'in the mood', or wait for inspiration to call you. Just write. Don't censor, don't judge; just see what comes out. Yes?

'I'm writing to you in some haste, but I want to let you know about a new theatre project called Centre 42. Its aim is to take exciting new plays around the country, to towns that don't have a permanent rep. theatre. They're offering a whole package: plays at town halls, local schools, church halls, etc., workshops for young people, and lunchtime poetry readings in factories. It smells slightly patronizing – taking Art to the Working Classes – but good people are involved. Arnold Wesker is one of the founders. It could be an interesting venture. What say you?

'I'm just off to a meeting of the Committee of One Hundred, which is now firmly established, amid much excitement. It's far more radical than CND, and plans to do more than hold ladylike marches to Aldermaston!

'Meanwhile, I'm still searching for rational reasons for believing in the absurd!

'Take care and do write soon.

  'Love,
    'Gerry.'

The third letter, the one with the South Wales postmark, I keep till last. But when I open it, I see it is not from Richard.

'Dear Danielle,

'I am not too well – perhaps nothing more than total exhaustion – and I'm finding it difficult to manage. We live in isolation here, rather cut off from the world, with few people to call upon. Richard thinks you may be willing to visit us? If you would come and stay with us for a while, and give me a hand with the children, it would be a great help.
'Thanks.
'Anna.'

Well! Well... The more I know, the less I understand; the more I think, the greater is my confusion. I am becoming more and more like Alice, lost in this perverse looking-glass world.

But Anna has set the seal on this seductive forbidden journey...

Journeys
Journeys of the feet
And of the heart
Beyond
Interior maps
Celestial guides
The heart of the universe
Beating
In my breast
Journeys…

Thirteen

Landscape tones: autumn gold brushing the countryside with endearments, green fields splashed egg-yoke yellow, sky slaked blue, pearl, violet; trees, half-naked, speckled burnt amber like an unfinished impressionist painting.

The train snakes through the fading smells of the turning world before it settles into winter sleep. Clouds squat with pregnant pride, waiting to hatch their icy rains; the wind whips up the dying passions of autumn. Nature in perpetual motion hints at omens of promise.

I, too, am dressed in the transitory colours of autumn, waiting to be renewed by the bright sting of winter, by your smile lighting up the end of the road. Migrating birds gather to gossip, swoop across my vision whispering confirmation on the wing. And I am hypnotized by the horizon galloping towards me, by the late October sun reminiscing on roof tops, by space foreshortened; all heralding belief.

The cliffs at journey's end rise up undaunted by time spilling from eternity, infusing memory with hope. Richard... arms pinioning me against parched summer earth, pithy voice loving me across rooms of other people, sleepy acquiescent grunts on tired nights when I wake you with lusty kisses. Laughing with me on streets cobbled with desire, tweaking my nipples in the bath, sitting on the tumbledown veranda breathing "Paradise Regained". Richard, with his pipe and his poetry, locked in a world of his own. Richard married to Anna.

Suddenly I am afraid. For what adumbrations of love await me in those four eyes that haunt me from across the mountains? Time speeds the train, which hurtles on regardless of my sensibilities, like the consequences of a bad decision. And I hang on, like a terrified child riding the Big Dipper at the fair, clutching desperately at enjoyment.

Autumn clouds roll back their disapproval, dispersing apprehension. For after all, it is Richard who will materialize out of the future to meet me: Orpheus ascending from the underworld. And not a thousand magnanimous wives can rob me of the miracle that will melt that moment. And the wrestling days that have undone my life and the screech owl recording my nightly tears and the redundant moon that has set each dawn unused, lie buried in the rubble of old rumours.

I am intoxicated by time on the move, by trees and fences and telegraph poles racing each other to the finishing post that they will never reach; by the world galloping by backwards. It collides with the past, but it cannot postpone the future. And I am hurtled on towards that event which too much anticipation has charged with disbelief.

I see Richard take my hand as we walk along uncompromising cliffs, as he teaches me to milk the goats, as we idle across fields, delirious with the abundance of life that will burst the veins of love if we do not hold our breath.

But in the doorway of your cottage I see not love's fulfillment hanging ripe with the birth of that moment, but Anna's shadow, a voluptuary question-mark rising through smoke clouds to mock expectancy with cautionary smiles; the brazen spectre of my fevered nights whom today my presence will vivify. Though I know she is there, ubiquitous, hurting me, even when I close my eyes. What eloquence can guide the confrontation and grant me absolution?

I open my eyes. I am afraid. For whom shall I be as I sit at your hearth, clutching at straws as at the air-drawn dagger?

I shall go back to the cottage. To my safe womb of loneliness. Familiar pain is easier to bear than untested fear. I shall pull the emergency cord and stop the train. But I see that it will pull down angels into the abyss before I can abort this pilgrimage.

What shall I do if the train stops, and I arrive?

* * * * * * *

I am covered in ash from too many cigarettes I didn't know I had been smoking. I brush my lap, and remember why I started to smoke. The bloated smile of the village shop-keeper looms uninvited into view, dissolves into my travelling companions, swaying blurred and tiny through the wrong end of my telescope. I am anaesthetized and cannot wake; in this drugged fog, the focus jumps.

'Would you like my cigarettes? Please take them; I've given up smoking. Just now.' I follow her middle-aged glance to my ash-covered clothes. Incredulity and suspicion take turns owning her face, and her mouth stutters words of hypocritical sociability. Why are such simple human gestures so charged with distrust?

But she doesn't take them, and the other passengers

don't smoke, or won't smoke Woodbines, so I throw them out of the window. And she looks at me as though *this* were the sin that opened Pandora's box. I stare back at the foliage on her hat, and wonder vaguely what would happen if I watered it.

'You see, I have a responsibility to the next generation.'

'Of course,' she says, smiling as one does to placate the half-mad, or pretend interest in a child's story one hasn't bothered to listen to. I look around the compartment, and wonder on which face I will see a mark of human kindness, resilience, grace; which eyes will reflect an amiable world. But the eyes and the faces are hidden behind newspapers, uneasy smiles, behind echoes of childhood voices that accost my ears; they don't understand, but they disapprove anyway. I slide back into tomorrow's reveries, self-indulgent, free from the untidy paraphernalia of existence.

* * * * * * *

Journeys outwards, inwards. Beyond... Physical journeys, to strange and other places; journeys of the inner eye. Seeking not new vistas, but new perceptions of old landscapes. New eyes to see what the world is hiding. Moving forward, inhabiting the future without fear. Paving reality by the way we walk our path.

Journeys... The aching voyage of the soul. Landmarks of love.

Will you journey with me? Will you be waiting for me when I arrive?

Will I arrive?

* * * * * * *

Suddenly, Cardiff stops the train and the end of my journey looms unstoppable as Judgement Day. But what defence shall I have against that moment of arrival, save the Word that Was in the Beginning, and a face of cosmetic courage?

On the crowded platform I wait for the local train. A bulging news-stand advertises the crowning achievements of mid-twentieth century civilization: ferocious massacres by the French in Dien Bien Phu, thousands die of cholera in India for want of a cheap Western drug, the Pope reaffirms his holy objections to birth control. Read all about it, understand the modern world, be up-to-date!

In the station cafe, I sip a cup of sweet plastic tea. The walls drip with the smells of cheap frying, transient laughter; of people passing through without their dreams. I am grateful for the synthetic small-talk of the overalled waitress. But how shall I get through the rest of time till I arrive?

Time: the devil's disciple. Time: desire measured in accelerated heartbeats.

I walk the length of the platform counting advertisements. I walk back again, seeing the same pair of lusty breasts beneath different faces, advertising sheer nylon stockings or shocking pink lipstick, or looking adoringly at the man with the new long cigarette for *real* satisfaction.

A toy engine puffs nonchalantly into the station and stops; Thomas the Tank Engine on weed. I furrow myself into a corner seat, excitement and trepidation tumbling over each other. And then the present dissolves in the fear of future insinuations.

Time holds its breath, punctuated only by my sudden incontinence and my need to comb my hair at five-minute intervals all through the half-hour journey.

* * * * * * *

And then we arrive, and Richard is waiting... I am in your arms, and everything is forgotten, and everything is remembered. Richard, embrace, pulsating, you, smell, lips, Richard, taste, tongues, you, touching, Richard, love, tightly, you, now, Richard... And I'm laughing and I'm crying and your arms suffocate me and your mouth is hard on my mouth and I Richard you we yes Richard Richard...

He puts my brown box suitcase and assorted carrier bags into an old wheelbarrow he has brought with him. He looks at my luggage, weighs up the implications, and smiles. Well, I don't know how long I've come for...

We dawdle along country lanes, wrapped around each other like spiral vines, our hands and our mouths covering each other with pent-up expectation. My heart beats so loudly I fear it will deafen the startled creatures darting through the undergrowth at our feet. We hold hands and stretch the twenty-minute walk to the limits of expedience.

And then his cottage – their cottage – slides into view. Richard squeezes my hand, then drops it like a live coal of culpability. Anna is standing there, La Gioconda framed in the cottage doorway. And this moment is all her, this dark *she,* whose shadow has haunted me through the long thirsting summer. *She* for whom I have died nightly and killed with my thoughts each day. She is standing three feet away from me, in the flesh; an incontrovertible fact.

And she is so entirely unexpected: her cropped tomboy haircut frames two enormous honey eyes; faded jeans and sweater, worn with the jaunty grace of the boss's daughter. She is slim and petite and looks about twelve years old. And her smile: a question mark, not a greeting.

She stands firmly planted on the earth, glowing with

the shocking assurance of one who truly knows her place. I take the proffered hand, but what am I to do with it? I am rooted to the spot. I want the ground to open up and swallow me. I want to escape, my fate; but then, whose fate should I inhabit? I attempt a smile, and hope it doesn't seem like an apology. I cannot look at Richard.

He takes my suitcase and bags, and *she* the scrag end of my self-confidence, into the cottage. Mute with misgiving, I follow them. Inside, Richard leads me up a stone staircase, along a low corridor to a tiny room, with a small latticed window and a narrow metal bed. Far too narrow for my chafing imagination. He puts down my case without looking at me.

'I'll leave you to unpack,' and he flees before weakness or my hands can change his mind.

Unpack? But what shall I unpack? Time? Memory? The smell of you folded inside my underwear? The arrogant folly that drove me to make this trip?

My suitcase, weighed down with aborted longing, is too heavy for me to lift. I sit on the bed and stare at it. If I open the lid, I'm not sure what will fall out.

I try to raise my sleeping courage and take it downstairs.

I sit with Richard and Anna at the old pine table in the stone kitchen. Their kitchen. Their home. I drink in this new reality with the cool tea that Anna serves me, willing it to transform itself, to be impregnable to the contrary will of others. I am buzzing with sharpened experience, but missing the links of comprehension.

I look for significance in every small action of Anna's: the way she tilts her glass, off-centre; the way she runs her left hand through the right side of her hair; her eyes, that seem to look at me round the corner of space. And when I don't find significance, I invent it. To my cost.

When at last I dare to lift my head, I see walls covered with Anna's huge abstract paintings, bold and bright and breathtakingly beautiful. Wooden shelves host uneven hand-made pottery, odd-sized re-used jars of herbs and spices, freshly baked bread. This room is all Anna: her smell, her struggle, her creativity. Earth mother, artist soul. I curl into my shame, swallowing the audacity of my journey. With one look from her glorious disconcerting eyes, Anna has upstaged us all. And I shall love her, for my suffering can offer her no less than love.

This moment that for so long has swollen my imagination with possibility, destroys itself around me; yesterday's delusions snuffed out by the spiky fingers of today's facts. Reality has become an Escher painting, evolving from fishes into birds before my eyes. Anna is no victim, not circumstance's nor anyone else's. Anna is her own creation; the hand that draws itself.

I sip my tea, the glass cupped between my hands like the last object of love, and wonder what could possibly have possessed me to come. But when Richard lights his pipe, drawing on it with those familiar sensuous movements, I know. Do we purchase our heart's desire at the cost of our soul? Then what am I being punished for? And worse, what am I punishing for?

I sit watching Richard who is watching Anna who is watching me, a revolving orgy of incommunicable desires. "Then let the barrier fall / In one circle have all..."

Soon it will be dark and I shall be forced to take off my sunglasses, my last protection against Anna's piercing eyes, against the evidence of my own panic. I shall be armed only with the memories I am struggling to create.

Excited voices burst into the room, arms and legs akimbo; childhood tumbling its up-side-down world into my apprehensions.

'Mummy, look, I picked you some berries...' 'Katie peed in her pants...' 'Did you make us some buns...' 'We built a new tree house and Robert says...' 'Who's that lady?' Arms and legs stop in mid-flight, as three pairs of curious eyes stare at 'that lady'. She manages a weak smile.

'She's a friend of ours; she's come to stay with us for a while. She's called Danielle.'

So I am named, 'a friend of ours'; and in that caressing definition, my defeat is complete.

* * * * * * *

Evening: the children are in bed; we have eaten and cleared away, and sit slowly drinking coffee. The first tensions are broken, though others rise up unceremoniously to replace them. The dull glow of the two oil lamps flickers an intimidating intimacy across the room. Only Anna, miscast, misread, misjudged Anna, is in control.

'Wouldn't you like to see the sea?'

'I... Well, I...'

'Why don't you go with Richard. I'd like an early night.'

Outside, the night is cool, but we are burning. We walk by the sea, the wild black sea foaming at the mouth; washing up new legends on the unsuspecting shore. But this legend is all ours, our joined mouths, the fabric of the night weaving around us its cloak of affirmation.

There is only the sea, moved by longing, tracing itself in the dark. And four eyes, gazing towards eternity...

Promise broken
And unbroken
Kisses revoked
Reinstated
The alchemy of longing
Gratitude
Skeleton dreams
Laid bare
Memories
Replanted
Under my skin...

Fourteen

In a small corner in the cracks of this make-believe paradise, I sit and look out at the world.

Leaves falling, heavy with late autumn; gold burnished smells of the earth fading into winter; time mapping the air with seasonal ciphers. The diminishing November sun writing footnotes to eternity...

My days are renewed here, tumbling over each other into the canvass of tomorrow's memory; alternating currents of atmospheres converging, dying, reborn. Irreverent cloudbursts washing away yesterday's ambivalence. The refuge that I'd roped together out of optimism and desperation, is knocked sideways; the scaffolding of facts distorting truth. But this new architecture, too, grants blessings.

During the long days, I take care of the children so that Anna can rest; and nurse that tiny new human who yet manages to whip up in me such an excrescence of emotions that I am overcome by confusion. This new baby, that was jumping for its life, while her father was planting other seeds...I melt with pain. I melt with love.

The children lead me by the hand across the rough

undergrowth. Down by the quarry, three small bodies refashion reality. The air is damp with the smell of hidden things. Wild pigweed, shepherds purse and meadowsweet grow bold and sprawl spiky secrets down towards the sea. Overhead, birds in dance formation stretch their wings towards warmer climes.

Round the corner of the horizon, distant rocks change from grey to purple, rise up massive like frozen figures trying to escape the ice age; then fall over the skyline into the sea. The wild distended sea, walls of waves walloping the cowering beach.

The villagers tell of a local man who drowned here, driven by despair when his wife ran off with the vicar, to throw himself off the cliffs. And now every year on that day the sea spits out a warning to the lovesick. And the parish priest preaches universal love in the name of Jesus.

The quarry is filled with old stones scarred with nature's ancient messages. The children play in the mud caught between crags; bog-myrtle and marsh marigolds push round the edges, queuing up to be kissed by the faint-hearted autumn sun.

From the raw clay, Robert moulds strange animals; creatures of satanic beauty with wild faces and long thin limbs, emerge from his prolonged concentration. He works with his whole body in continuous movement, a dance choreographed by the Muses and the seed of his father's passion. I cannot take my eyes off him.

When they are finished, he places his figures in a half-circle, a tableaux of mystic meaning. He stares at them a long moment, caught up in some private runic dialogue. Then with one lithe movement he crushes his creations between strong fingers and tosses them back into the quarry. Hands of an artist, child-mind; only adults, fearful of time rushing dreams into regrets, need to preserve a legacy.

His work done, Robert starts back across the fields; the two little girls in tow, handmaidens to the crown prince. We come out in a clearing of sparse foliage, encircled by ancient trees and scattered stones: pagan shrine, or perhaps modern picnic site. We watch the Martians land and explore their spaceship hovering above the shrubs. We dig deep into the marshy earth to find Jules Verne's submarine and, behind the boulders, Indians and cowboys fight over old gold. The two little girls, wearing Anna's genes, are feisty.

Katie asks why her mummy hasn't come to play with them. Robert says, "'Cos she's feeding baby Jess.'

'Why hasn't my daddy come?'

'Cos he's busy working.'

'Why?'

'He makes words, and he plants them and they grow into poems.'

Katie considers this, then stares at me. 'Why is *she* here?'

Robert shrugs, seeing absolutely no reason for my presence. Joanna says, 'I like her,' and gives me a hug. I say, 'What shall we play now?'

Robert looks up at the sky. 'The goats are hungry.'

And so we go to feed the goats. The children teach me to milk them, and laugh at my clumsiness. ['I take your hand and walk with you to find the goats... And I show you how to milk, and watch you laugh... '] And now I am here with your children, your love with another made flesh. And I am laughing. What duplicitous games are the gods playing, with my reluctant acquiescence?

It starts to rain. In moments, the aluminium sky swells up, bruise blue; clouds break apart, unleashing their pent-up passions. Soaked to the bone and out of breath, we sprint back to the cottage and some of

Anna's comforting hot stew.

* * * * * * *

This meanwhile space suspends all thought, shapes metaphors I dare not explore. Angels with treasonous eyes are wooing me with honeyed smiles to cheat the flowering sympathy of deception. And God speaks with a forked tongue.

I watch the children playing hide-and-seek among the haystacks and the trees beyond. These sturdy old oaks, heavy with wisdom, witness to hundreds of years of gushing time and human foibles, bend their branches to accommodate the children's games. Katie hides and does not want to be found.

And I am truly lost. With one eye on a book, I try to analyze the fate that has entrapped me. Detached from my ego, indifferent as a statistician reeling off the thousands dead, I dissect the wheels of manipulation. But after all what am I but a hungry cat, howling at your lighted window for the mangy scraps you drop from your table?

And then I see Anna working too hard, while you cloister yourself upstairs making poetry, or sit drinking coffee with a 'do not disturb' sign carved across your brow; and I am upset that you do not do more to help her. And I renounce my love for you, only out of solidarity for her.

But then you come out of hiding, and brush my arm in passing, and my nerves jangle to attention, and every cell in my body succumbs to this wild and dizzying thrill. And I know that all the cold instruments of thought are only another defence against those protracted hours that pass without your touch.

I am fatally wounded with the seeds of love.

* * * * * * *

Early morning birdcalls shuffle off sleep. Dawn, overtaking the sky, breaks open my room, milky with new expectations. The house still sleeps, maybe dreams... I get up to make breakfast, to surprise my hosts with my diligence. But biology thwarts even such simple endeavours: overcome by nausea, I spew my guts across the landing.

Anna puts a cool hand on my arm and leads me back to bed. She looks at me. She knows. How simple. Choking with sobs and vomit, I grapple with the muscles of my conscience not to throw myself into her lap. I need her comfort; I resent the moral highground she commands.

'Does Richard know?'

I shake my head. If I open my mouth to speak I do not know what I shall retch up.

'It is his child, isn't it?' Hardly a question. I nod.

Anna is dignified. She offers help; she does not intrude. I squeeze her hand, too hard for gratitude. We sit in terrible silence, neither of us able to move. She seems to argue with herself, unsure whether to speak or hold her counsel. Then she smiles, a luminous smile, full of thought.

'It's so hard to move forward at all, to make any sense of life. We waste so much energy on nonsense; on ambitions and goals and all the other neuroses of our culture conditioning. When really life is simple, joyous. I suppose if we are open, allowing...

'You sound like Richard.' But I didn't know whether I was praising or damning her.

'Well, we've lived together for ten years!' Her voice is gentle, confiding secrets to a valued friend. How did I come to be playing this role? 'We've shared every intimacy – physical, emotional, spiritual I suppose. It's been hard, at times desperately hard, but also rewarding. I've journeyed a long way; both with him, and in our battles, through him!'

I look at her in wonder. Does Richard not know the strength of this extraordinary woman? Cerebral yes, but so much more: powerful and beautiful and radiantly alive. Whose paint-box did he use to colour her as pedestrian and compliant? Mine, perhaps.

'"Yesterday this day's Madness did prepare / Tomorrow's silence, Triumph, or Despair: / Drink; for you know not whence you came, nor why..."'

'The Rubaiyat?'

'It's time I thanked you for it.'

One misplaced heroic gesture...

'You know, when you arrived, I was intimidated by you too. You looked so formidable behind your long shawl and dark glasses. I wanted to know what your eyes were hiding.' She smiles gently. 'And I thought how much you have to give; how soft you are. I'm not very good at giving any more.'

'Anna ...' But I cannot lie to her, and the truth is unspeakable.

And at that moment I knew, deeply and unfathomably, that although I am now the more loved by Richard, I am also the more dispensable.

* * * * * * *

One afternoon, Richard is not working... We walk to the small cove overlooking the bay, and watch the sky play hide-and-seek with the clouds. The earth is green and brown and golden. And a little damp, but I don't mind too much. And you give me that for which there are no words. Then you kiss my eyes, feather light, and brush the grass out of my hair, and say, 'You are the one...'

Love is strong as death.

* * * * * * *

Tell me, what shall be born from this triangular womb? What stories carved by this unholy trinity of lovers? I muse on the changing weights of silence, beyond interpretation. I try to hide behind the accessories of others' lives. I buy temporary salvation.

During the day the children look after me, teaching me new games to dispel old hurts. Nature and the wild outdoors is their school; the classroom has yet to interrupt their education. They teach me the names of flowers and trees and shrubs, the movement of birds, the habitats of insects. They are astonished at my ignorance. So am I.

Sometimes, we help Anna to bake bread or make yoghurt and cream cheese from sour goat's milk dripping in muslin bags over the kitchen sink. Sometimes the children draw, using charcoal from the dying embers of yesterday's fire. Or they make wondrous objects from whatever the earth offers them that day: startling birds poised to fly off the ground at any moment, strange faces carved in wood bark, a medieval city made from honeycombs. Joanna made me a daisy-chain and I cried.

But in the long oil-lit hours of darkness, when I sit sharing silence with Anna, Richard's protracted absence gnaws into my flesh. The insistent tapping of his typewriter bangs out its rhythmic treachery from his ivory tower above our heads. His once potent instrument of love now bangs out new codes to defeat biology; answers to questions that no-one has asked. And Rome burns.

I look up for the hundredth time. Anna catches my look, involuntarily stretches her hand towards me, draws back; for my sake. I smile, sadness and love.

Beware, my darling. For though you may play at being puppeteer, you cannot tie up the threads of your life in such neat knots of compliance. And while you dangle upstairs with your metallic mistress, other alliances are formed, and smiles of complicity blossom without your acquiescence.

'How dare he presume that his poetry is more important than your painting!' Than my lips.

Anna laughs. 'Intellectually he demolishes sexism, of course; but he hides behind the unconscious privilege of his gender. A biblical patriarch; benign, but still a dictator!'

'How do you – ' But I couldn't finish the question. This is, after all, Richard I'm talking about. With his wife!

'There are lean times, but also good times. Journeys. Children. Conversation. Our lives are – enmeshed. A bizarre symbiosis perhaps; obstinate, as we are. But enduring. We work it out.'

And where does this leave me? She takes my hand; warm, inclusive. Anna, I love you. For you. Why did you have to be Richard's wife?

I hadn't noticed that the tapping above my head had ceased. Richard is standing in the doorway. He looks at each of us, at our joined hands, which we do not relinquish. It is the first time I have ever seen him lose his composure. He is jealous; but I'm not sure of whom.

* * * * * * *

I walk with Richard along the cliffs. The sadness of the sea below saturates my senses. We walk in silence, 'the long sea relentlessly grinding the pebbles...' I am afraid...

'I – I have something to tell you.'

'I wondered when.'

'I'm going to have a child.'

'Yes.'

'How – When did you... ?

'When you arrived. Your face wore that look, a kind of mystic knowing, that pregnant women have.'

'What shall I do Richard?'

'You shall have a child. You will be a mother. The most beautiful, most powerful, most deeply spiritual experience a woman can have.'

'And what will you do?

'I shall be a father.'

He turns me to face him, and kisses my eyes, so tenderly, so tenderly, closing them with love. And then he kisses my lips, tasting of a new respect. And sealing my silence.

Then he takes my hand and we walk back along the jutting cliffs. A brooding sky breathes dark omens overhead. Winter enters my heart.

Later, alone, I fret frustration at his gentle manipulation. At his kisses that bought my silence. At all my unasked questions...

* * * * * * *

Richard borrows a hay-cart and takes Anna to the village; from there a bus to the hospital, where she is to stay for a while. Last time, she robbed me of twelve days of my life, of Richard; and caused me to stir up such a cauldron of Machiavellian thoughts that I wait every moment for the coming wrath of God. But perhaps the waiting is the punishment.

I watch them till they fall over the horizon, Richard's arm around her shoulders, beaming the protective. She looks back and smiles, her daunting honey eyes looking at me and through me with total trust.

I gather up the children for a long walk by the sea; a wild sea, balm to a troubled spirit. I walk over to the cliffs and sit on the edge, the edge of an otherwise life for which I can find no key. I watch the sea, washing up wave after wave of watery enigma. And I think how easy it would be... How final. But the winter sun smiles bravely, enticing me. Not now. I have the children to mind.

My reflection changes, and a gentle hermaphrodite gazes back, with seaweed smiles and collusive wink. And nothing is but what is not.

What will happen? Nothing. For everything has already happened. And Anna has robbed me of the will to hope.

* * * * * * *

Anna's absence is everywhere, filling the space between us, demanding from us more than her presence ever acknowledged. Oh my darling, isn't this what we dreamed of on the other side of experience? But dreams are for dreaming, and when circumstance connives to provide their fulfillment, the fulcrum has moved. Beware of what you wish for!

Richard takes time from his work, and we sit in the gorse watching the children play.

'Robert says you love my daddy.'

'Shut up Jo.'

Robert, the father's son incarnate; Robert, Joanna's nine-year-old god.

Richard's eyes bore holes through the back of my head and the role thrust upon me.

'But Robert is right. I do love your daddy. And your mummy. I love all of you.'

'Come, let's go in and eat.' And Richard gathers us up as though for all the world we were one big happy family.

* * * * * * *

We lie on Richard's bed, fully clothed. Anna lies

between us, a palpable throb, heavy, immovable. Her shadow laughs softly in the darkness.

Richard turns towards me. 'I want to tell you a story. According to an ancient folk tale, when the gods created the world, they argued about where to hide Truth. It had to be far away, for humans would only appreciate what they had searched for long and hard. One god suggested that Truth should be hidden at the top of the highest mountain. Another suggested, on the farthest star. A third, at the bottom of the deepest ocean. When all the gods had exhausted all their possibilities, the oldest and wisest of them spoke: "No. We shall hide Truth in the heart of each human being."' Richard smiles his enigmatic smile. 'The journey to the heart is a long one.'

'The Kabbalah tells that when God had finished creating the world – the sky, the seas, the earth, the plant and animal kingdoms – he looked upon his handiwork, and it found favour in his eyes. So he decided that he would make a dwelling place for himself on earth. And so he created human beings, to dwell within their hearts.' I smile. 'God wins over truth.'

'God is Truth.' His eyes tease; but hold serious intent.

Two weeks ago, we sat up all night talking, curled up on your downy pillows, dancing round the edges of that embrace where artistic creation and spiritual aspiration meet. Then, with Anna and the baby asleep in the next room, we were alone on earth. Now, Anna's absence insinuates itself between us, whispering in the dark...

Two weeks ago, we traced each other's biography of love; melting skin, indelible spill of longing. We created new histories that would appear in no texts; a new religion of silent mutual worship. And like the ancient Jewish rabbis talking all night of God, we were unaware of the passing time, until a grey dawn nudged uninvited at the window-pane.

'I should go back to my room.'

Richard took my face between his hands and lightly kissed my nose. 'My sweet little Danielle, still thinking of propriety?'

'No. Not for propriety's sake, for Anna's.' Or perhaps for mine, to be able to hold her gaze when her taunting eyes would undress mine.

But that was two weeks ago. Tonight I cannot talk. I am undone with words. Tonight there's a full moon. I start to cry. Oh love, love, what shall I be without you? I don't even own our past; the taste of memories stolen from my mouth.

Richard rolls over Anna's shadow. 'Dearest heart, you know that you will not be without me. Wherever you are, wherever I am.'

'Yes, yes. But I want *you*, Richard. Not metaphysical word play! You, in the flesh.' [Dear God, in the flesh...] 'It's easy for you; you have everything.'

You stare at me, so long, so hard, that I wither in that look that holds my life in the balance. Then you say, 'Yes, you are right. If you think that everything can exclude the woman I love.'

There were no more words. Until a long time later, and I said, 'Which one of us should tell Anna about tonight?'

* * * * * * *

Anna has come back to us. She steps from the ambulance smiling, extends a hand to each of us. The moment locks itself around us; the circle is closed.

Richard takes her case, and I smile, remembering... We sit in the large stone kitchen sipping cool tea round the old pine table. Anna's kitchen; and I am wearing faded jeans and sweater. But no sunglasses.

Anna is well and her health has robbed me of all excuse to stay. I live here vicariously, on borrowed time. The days have spread languidly into weeks, and I have postponed all thought of the future; all thought.

But my changing shape creates new realities, different demands. "The circle has run its dull and fevered race..." The future rises up on the edge of the horizon, terrifying as a nightmare from which one can not wake, painted all the garish colours of inevitability.

'Anna, it's – it's time to go.' I have no idea how I shall accomplish this; how I shall make my legs move out of the door. One step at a time, I suppose, like climbing Everest.

Anna is gracious. She thanks me for being here.

'"Only in lasting sleep is there a rest from jealousy." To misquote Philaster,' she adds. Then she embraces me, a hug from the heart. I could not believe that Anna could love me. I could not have been more astonished had Richard suggested eloping with me to Las Vegas.

* * * * * * *

I steal Richard for one last day. When I was little, the birthday girl ruled for the day, playing out wild fantasies, 'casting' the rest of the family in her play. But midnight always struck; the soldier, free for the day for his one good deed on earth, is taken back to purgatory.

I run through the bracken, and Richard chases me, with wild calls. Yes, Richard, I have taught you to be young again. And you have forced me to grow up. We come out on to the cliff that overhangs the bay. Our cove...

'Richard, I'm leaving. Tomorrow. Oh Richard, love

me, love me one more time… Richard…'

'Danielle, my darling, I…' But my mouth is hard on your mouth, and all the restrained passion of long days and nights of abstinence unleash…

When the earth is still again, we lie together watching the sea rise up to embrace the sky. And you caress my face and kiss my eyes and postpone the hurt that will engulf me when I leave. The greater hurt is not always left behind.

And we love again, with infinite tenderness, with the exquisite agony of protraction. And we lie folded in each other's arms, a last attempt to enfold the world between us. And you trace your fingers gently across my gravid belly, and I cry.

"Stand still you ever moving spheres of heaven / That time may cease…"

But time takes no account of human desires, and dusk, stealthy as a practised thief, overtakes us. Weighed down with the unbearable sadness of being, we move back into the world.

* * * * * * *

The Last Supper. But who will give the Judas kiss?

We play out our predetermined roles. But there are no words; there is too much to say. Just smiles weeping sorrow, Anna's steadfast eyes, and Richard watching me and watching me in the protean shadows. No-one wants to break the spell, to go to bed.

Dawn breaks over the silent house, blows the half-sleep from my eyes. Now that I am going, I want to be gone. I want to be the other side of parting.

The three of us stand by the door, holding hands; the circle is complete. The taxi driver lights a cigarette, watching, quizzical. Perhaps he knows…

'Where will you go?'

Where will I go? Into the nothingness of a black hole. Despair. Scrummaging in the dark for fragments of the scattered debris of love. Retracing memory, no longer my own. Drowning in your absence. Drowning..

I say, 'London. Friends.'

'Friends?'

'Beth. You will visit me?'

'Of course...'

I step outside the circle and leave, to be haunted forever by those four eyes gazing at me, beyond me... "When shall we three meet again..." But my battle is already lost.

Cushioned in the belly of the taxi, I allow myself a backward glance: Richard and Anna, held together by tattered but invincible ropes of symbiosis. And six-year-old Joanna, rushing out, waving her arms wildly, screaming after me in the wind to come back soon.

Earthing illusion
Butterfly breath
Transformation
Your night sighs
Cradling the world
In a crib
For our unborn
Child…

Fifteen

'No end, no beginning. Only the Word, indivisible by time.' Words written to me in a previous incarnation. By my lover, in a previous incarnation.

The circle is broken; its revolution, history. I cannot go back; and towards the future, what way is there? I am strung up between worlds, my woundedness tracing my biography of loss. And all of danger's fulfillment cannot rewrite even one insignificant narrative.

I stare at the world, eyes bloodshot with sorrow. And the world stares back, but weeps no pity in its third eye. Shall I also, through the detours of nihilism, find my way to God?

Obeying the grim command of litter notices, I have left nothing behind. Only my footsteps, intractable, and the cause of my riven love. "The Cause, my soul..." The mantra of my life.

The weeks spent writing the future's prologue with our lives are left hanging across the Welsh mountains like yesterday's washing, blowing in the wind. Without answers. A brief interlude to spice some dinner-party gossip or a dull lecture on the Human Potential of

Love; a footnote in someone else's text.

I have come to the edge of the ocean; the watershed of waste. The sea has parted and I have crossed through. And the waves have closed behind me. But no-one will come after me to tempt me back, with gifts of God or mammon. And the wilderness waiting on the far shore will not lead me to the Promised Land.

British Rail, oblivious to the heartache riding its carriages, hurtles me towards my metropolitan future. I rattle with the train, a sack of old bones, unburied. A bird of prey with large black wingspan darkens the low-slung winter sky outside the window; an omen of menace, threatening as Death.

Richard's words gnaw at my heart: 'The spirit will find us out precisely in that place of deep darkness. For it is there that we have most need of redemption. It is there that we may begin to grow.' But I won't go there. The wounds are too fresh. And I wrap myself more tightly in my worn-out cloak of regret.

The train rumbles on: de-de-de de, de-de-de de, the relentless beat of a rhythm with no heart. I clutch at a few crusty crumbs of consolation: it was, after all, my decision to leave, if not my choice. And armed with this mischievous fact, I race my thoughts across the West Country.

Trains: childhood memories, selected, sieved, sanitized. Summer trains, shuttling between mother and father, separated by blighted hopes and too many recriminations. Journeys from London to Manchester; imagination on the wing. Reality suspended, five hours of nowhere on the move: my time, between time, belonging to no-one, the world belonging to me. Forlorn in my small reserved corner, disfigured by shyness, I would peep out at the world through lost child eyes. But no-one could steal my ten-year-old fantasies: I am really a princess, disguised in raggledy clothes for my own amusement; to see who is kind. Magical moments, lived in parentheses.

The scarred membrane of childhood, bandaged by adult's regret; punished for usurping the adults' lost dreams. The monotone of the record stuck inside my head: wash your hands eat your supper don't pick your nose kiss your auntie Miriam do as you're told stop asking why go to bed like a good little girl.

But a good little girl I was never able to be. It broke my mother's heart more often than the dishes I threw in my uncontrollable rages. I could never attain this image of acceptability, served up with over-cooked vegetables at every meal. It crippled my spirit; I limped through childhood with leg-irons on my soul.

Memory: future scars, carved in my image. My unborn child will also commute between mother and father, between here and there, between home and away; crossing invisible borders between realities rendered by others. Fantasies spin tangled webs, stamped with the imprint of the next generation. But for now you are cosseted in the womb of time, growing inside me, feeding off my body, feeding my soul. I shall paint a glorious new world for you, my darling. But shall I be strong enough to let you brave it alone? For you are the only mirror of Richard's eyes that will smile to me in tomorrow's time-blind looking-glass.

A uniformed attendant appears, pushing a trolley of plastic food that tempts no-one's taste buds. But people buy anyway: cellophane sandwiches and salty crisps to be washed down by powdered coffee and milk that never saw a cow.

The train thunders on, scuttling my nerves towards London and the panic that threatens to engulf my arrival. My grief-soaked mind travels to some distant place without me. To that other journey, of the feet, of the heart... Now, the pain knocks inside my skull; it shrieks with the wheels of the train, piercing as the wail of ten thousand war widows; of one.

I do not notice nature's change of clothes, nor the pristine villages we casually bisect as we rush towards progress at sixty miles an hour. I rock with the rhythm of the train, with the rhythm of my own cracking heart.

* * * * * * *

So through the winter landscape my future reorders itself, and apprehension weighs me down more heavily than my changing shape. Mother dear, how shall I face your sorrow, which will burn holes through my swelling stomach? For though I may try to hide the love in my eyes to save your blushes, nothing can disguise its half-grown purpose.

Sudden images of my parents scatter the storm clouds scurrying past the windows, and I melt with love, with remorse. For whom shall I be as I return to visit you but the prodigal daughter, limping sheepishly homewards, with guilt writ large across my forehead like the mark of Cain? Knowing I have nothing to offer you but disappointment to clothe your weary old age.

The old arguments buzz through my pounding head, lining up stubborn as weeds pushing through cracked paving stones, to taunt my failing courage, to protect them from the truth.

'What's all this talk about the theatre? Get yourself a proper job, till you get married.' 'You could join the local Jewish amateur dramatic group. They do some nice shows, I believe.' But I stood, defiance massed against them, and my father tried a gentler bait: 'Daneleh, you're a clever girl. Go to university first; have something to fall back on.'

But those with nunnery minds will not understand the holiness of passion, nor a thesaurus with no word for compromise. I became an actress, and made non-Jewish friends [friends?] and worked on the Sabbath. And the sky did not fall on my head. Flushed with conviction, I longed to lay at their feet the excitement of my new world; the many blessings unknown in a synagogue. But I could not: the price of their approval was my perjury. And all the while my parents knew that the worst was yet to come.

And now, a wayward waif of raw vulnerability, I struggle home in the dark, weighed down with suitcases of memories...

The outskirts of our capital city rise through distant smog to offer an indifferent welcome: red double-decker buses, industrial smoke, a teeming metropolitan hive buzzing with busy bees that manage never to touch each other. An accident of geometry, or have we learnt the codes too well?

Paddington station: the bees have grown larger and are heaving into human shape. Do I also wear the casual mask of those who rush about disguised as people? The ticket collector takes in my ticket and my condition with a leery smile; he looks as though he knows what it's for.

Plus ça change... London has not missed me. I lower my head and scurry through the detritus of last night's partying humanity. And I fear not that I am so different, but that I could too easily be the same.

Behind the station, a horde of hungry cats squeal as they savage bloody fish heads thrown out by the fish and chip shop. I shudder at their butchery and hurry away to hide in the twilight zone of the tube.

But at the entrance, I am overcome by terror. I can not face the dark descent into the underworld, tunnels snaking through the great belly of Pluto lit up like a brilliant clockwork nightmare. So I take a taxi I cannot afford, and revel in the luxury of this dark-windowed cocoon from which I may look out at the world that cannot look in on me.

Across London, neon signs wink relentlessly; but illuminate nothing.

* * * * * * *

Beth's flat is a comforting clutter of newspaper cuttings, cigarette butts, old demonstration posters, scattered cushions and people, half-drunk mugs of coffee, a jungle of books from Trotsky to Carl Jung. And the old cat that Beth, in a moment of weakness, had named Oedi-puss, walking with equal disdain over poetry and people.

People leave. Beth and I sit by the fire, drinking cocoa. I make Beth talk about herself, because I want to hear, because I don't want to talk; because I need to buy time to arm' myself against her censure. She tells me that she's phoned Gerry, and he's delighted I've come home.

Home? This hypocrisy of a word trips lightly off her tongue, but without malice. Once indeed it had been home, and it has not changed. I feel unfaithful, a schizophrenic who's other self has made love with her own husband. The focus has moved, and I am bound like Prometheus with chains of suffering to that centre of all homes...

Beth is cool and twenty-four and has intellectual friends. She loves me. She thinks I've made a fine mess of things. She does not censure.

Beth's boyfriend turns up around midnight and I crawl off to my room, swathed in loneliness. I sink into the tattered rocking-chair, a faded family heirloom that smells of warmth, of my grandmother, of strong arms to take away childhood hurts. I close my eyes and rock wistfully, the anaesthetic of *booba's* lullaby humming through my body. But childhood's sanctuary cannot assuage adult desolation.

I walk around the room, touching the young woman I'd left behind: a blind person's need for contact; a child's reassurance that the world will still be there tomorrow. My books, the slow measure of my changing tastes and concerns; pottery mugs; old Chinese print; the impish grandfather clock ticking away a time of his own.

This room breathes old aspirations, the beginnings of dreams... It belongs to a young girl, full of passions, ambitions, causes. But the woman who has returned can find no synthesis. Now I see the exact measure of my confinement, but the walls offer no clues. They drip despair and mournfully beg only another coat of paint.

I unwrap Anna's parting gift: a pen and ink drawing she made for me of Richard. I hang it above my bed. In place of a crucifix.

The world will never be the same again.

* * * * * * *

I telephone my parents first to warn them, to try to dilute their expectation at my longed-for homecoming. But what misrepresentation of truth can I offer them to sugar this pill? What atonement can acquit me of the murder of their optimistic prayers?

But though I am anointed with the crown jewels of love, the sight of my parents' house still stabs me with remorse, with ruth. My childhood home rising through mists of suburban nostalgia to claim me. Brooding familiarity: shabby, cluttered, defeated by compromise and struggle. No provocation could alter this house, nor my parents' steadfast prejudices.

My mother gushes over me as she ushers me into the small over-furnished sitting room.

'So you've left the theatre. We knew you'd come to your senses. We knew you'd come home.'

And my father smiles knowingly, as though he's won a battle he hadn't fought.

'Well don't just stand there. Take off your coat.'

I fumble with the buttons, with the last remnants of my failing courage. I twist my hair nervously round my fingers. I falter on the altar of familial obligation.

My mother takes my coat and then stops mid-track, her feet glued to this pregnant pause. Horror and disbelief dissolve her face, and her eyes like hounded ghosts mirror the suffering of centuries of Jewish motherhood.

'Mama, I love him.'

She sobs and tugs at her hair and demands of God to know where she has failed.

'How could you? How could you do this to us? We should never have let you go. I knew no good would come of it. How could you? What kind of wedding can we make now?'

I try to close my ears to her accusations, but they stab through my flagging resolve. Spit it out, Danielle. Before your nerve ruptures.

'There isn't going to be any wedding. He's married.'

She weeps and wails and beats her breast and rants at the slippery claws of her ebbing authority over a life she thought she owned. I look to my father, more worldly and intelligent than she. But the silent censure in his inflexible eyes tears me to shreds; is harder to bear.

But there is no going back: old prayers cannot answer new necessities. I will not defend myself by invoking That Word, debased by mindless pop-singers and sanctimonious preachers. And I will not ask forgiveness for a sin I do not recognize.

I stand rooted at the edge of this moment. I cannot look at them, my beloved parents, whose distraught faces I can never cease to love. I weep for their pain also; broken people, beyond solace, who had returned to each other in middle age, seeking through loneliness what they had not found through love. Now they have only the decaying clutches of biology to feed their dwindling days.

Suddenly I catch sight of the old brass candlesticks, solemn in their sacrosanct place on the mantelpiece. And the image of my mother, when I was a child, blessing the Sabbath candles, and then my father blessing me and my sister... This desolates me more than their haunted glazed eyeballs that now see nothing but devastation. The eye of childhood paints their faces with rose-tinted features, and I weep also for the little girl inside me who has died.

My young sister averts her eyes from her fallen god, but the back of her cropped head bristles accusations, and reminds me of those times when I was big and she was little and she would cry to be left behind when I went out. But now, little sister, you are big too, and in spite of a broken heart you will find ways to defend me when your fifteen-year-old friends jeer and call me 'whore.'

But she slams out of the room, and her sobs shake the foundations of the house, as well as of my failing nerve.

I cross the room to embrace my mother, but she stiffens and turns away, and says she never wants to see me again. It is this gesture that finally cuts the umbilical cord. And when she relents months – aeons – later, this ungiven kiss fills the heaviness between us, and claims the hypocritical tear.

My father walks me to the door and stands, head bowed, for eternity, as though he doesn't want the torment to end. When he finally looks at me, I see in his eyes the child he had loved, displaced forever by a gaping defeat. He looks away, crushed, and offers me money – the only thing he would allow himself to give. The only thing I could not accept.

Outside, I want to melt into the snow and burn away the silent hurt of those eyes that will haunt me forever.

* * * * * * *

Beth is out all day being bright at her glossy magazine, and I am left alone with my misery and the cat. Outside my curtained window the street groans with the weight of life, without my acquiescence: children go unwillingly to school, secretaries with lipstick smiles slave to leery-eyed bosses, house-trained bank clerks struggle to balance their ledgers with one eye on the clock. And cats scream as they perform that act I cannot name.

In the evening, the flat becomes a hive of inactivity: Beth's literary friends, politicos, the odd academic or painter, drop in to sprawl untidily across the floor, drinking wine and playing music and lustily re-ordering the world. From far away, I watch this gentle distraction of Swiss Cottage life: pleasant people who accept me as I am and make no demands, not even that my silences be friendly.

No action claims me, seduces me with even fleeting temptation; every prospect the world can offer frowns only futility. I smile incomprehension at the busy world that takes itself so seriously; Paddington bees... I shall go to bed and stay there: it is as good a place as any to lie and brood and wait unceremoniously to hatch.

But oh, my baby is burning volcanoes through the menacing fact, and cries untimely for her awakening, which is also mine. All my dreams course with blood, are stalked by ghosts of he whose child is struggling inside me. And then they dissolve, and the silence breeds terrors more terrible than any nightmare. Future lullabies are drowned in hurricanes of despair. All sacrifice is in vain.

But Reality, that sophisticated party-goer, again gatecrashes my life: Beth gets the flu, and I am forced to nurse her instead of my grief. So I play at being housewife, and try to muster the necessary diligence. But Beth is grumpy and snivelling and admonishes me for feeding us for three days on warmed-up rice and raspberry yoghurt. I am offended; I did my best.

Beth gets better – and worse: she forces me with wily ruses to succumb to worldly distractions. I go to the cinema. One week, indulging my own brand of masochism, I see Bergman's "Seventh Seal" another three times. If I take up chess, perhaps I shall also meet with Death. The next week I go every day to the News Cinema in Baker Street, and laugh my tears away with Tom and Jerry.

I go to the bank to draw money and the teller says, 'Your account is in the red.' And I think, now everything I touch turns to rivers of blood. So I get a job typing envelopes at home, which breaks my nails, and very nearly the camel's back as well.

Beth is trying to help. She feeds me, and talks to me, and tries to dissuade me from reading Sartre. She says I should concentrate on the sensible. But Sartre underwrites my state of mind, busy with the nature of being and nothingness. I stroke the cat and think, Beth *is* kind. But I can't take it anyway.

* * * * * * *

My friends are concerned. They plan ingenious strategies to beguile me back into the world of the living. But there is only one antidote to my loneliness, and he is sitting two hundred [two million] miles away, typing odes to save a world that doesn't want to be saved.

So I sit in the middle of the floor hugging my knees to my swelling belly, rocking myself incessantly to the rhythm of this murderous lullaby of pain and thinking that maybe I shall die in childbirth.

Or else I sit on the bed eating oranges and cutting faces from the peels and then I stop eating but I go on peeling and cutting and we live on orange juice orange salad orange mousse for a week.

Or else I sit in the ancient rocking chair stroking my old stuffed doll Crosspatch, who's lost one eye and seen better days, and try to tempt Oedi-puss to play with me. But even the cat disdains my company and I am left rolling the cotton reel alone.

Beth has given up finding me jobs to do since instead of cleaning I wrote 'RICHARD' across the furniture in the dust and then I took her lipstick and wrote his name on all the mirrors and windows and then I took the flour and wrote 'RICHARD' huge and white across the kitchen floor. Now she wears a glazed look, and brings me my meals in bed.

Some days, when the constellation of the planets is agreeable, I get out of bed and go for a walk. I tramp the streets, and fancy I see a conciliatory mask upon the face of the world. But it fades as I approach, into mocking glances, confusion, into its perpetual preoccupation with the busyness of living.

I stop at a newsagent and buy six pennyworth of distraction. The pictures in the papers are of wars and refugees and bloody revolutions and a local child kidnapped and murdered. And I mourn for a world run amok in pursuit of greed and power and senseless violence. I count my blessings, as I did as a child when told to by my mother: one blessing, two blessings, three blessings… And go back to bed.

* * * * * * *

The meeting is at Paula's flat, a basement converted from a home for rats and bats and things that go bump in the night, to an almost des. res. in Pimlico.

I know most of the women, sitting on assorted mattresses and cushions on the floor. The smell of courage and vulnerability, of harsh passions and burning ideals, of women struggling to seize control of their lives, punctures my nostrils. It's good to reconnect.

Posters from recent demonstrations are scattered on all available surfaces: "The Personal is Political", "My Body Belongs to Me", "Rape is a Political Weapon". But a photograph of a baby in its mother's arms holding up a placard, "I am a wanted baby", sends me rushing to the john to steady my nerves. I sit on the lid of the toilet, shaking with warring emotions. On the mirror someone has scrawled in pink lipstick: *"You are beautiful as you are"*. And by the basin below it, a ceramic bowl grows heavy with gifts of discarded make-up.

This is one of the early Consciousness Raising groups, where we grapple to understand the political roots of our oppression as women. Men, the perpetrators of this oppression, have become the enemy. A hesitant voice, who blames the system rather than the opposite sex, is followed by an uneasy silence. We are the pioneers of the new embryonic wave of feminism, and we are painting in bold strokes, not fine lines. We plan strident strategies to break free of our chains, and sweep up all obstacles with the same brash brush.

We share intimate experiences and begin to see

wider implications. We don't admit that inside we are raw, hurting, emotionally vulnerable. We are tough, striding in the shoes of the early suffragettes. This is no time for niceties.

Three new women have joined the group in my absence and Paula is anxious to introduce me.

'Dani is a hero! She has chosen to become a single mother. We applaud you, Dani.' And they do.

But I am not a hero. I am a fraud. My maternity top hides my aching heart as well as my bulging stomach. My baby is the fruit of love, not a political statement.

I love these women. I admire their tenacity, their stubborn courage, the honesty of their struggle. But I do not belong here. Yet reconnecting with them, or rather with my old self that is drawn to them, has nudged my perception of 'Richard as rescuer' sideways. But nothing can dent my longing.

Richard, when will you remind me that what I ache for will again fill my nights? Is to be believed.

* * * * * * *

Beth and Alan are taking his kid to the zoo. They want to take me too. They are kind. But I can't bear Sundays, so I pull the covers more tightly over my head, and hope they'll go away and take the day with them. But Beth wrenches the covers away and says curtly, 'Don't you think you're guarding your suffering a little too zealously?' She closes the door behind her and I cry uncontrollably. Then I get up and go with them to the zoo.

* * * * * * *

And then a small brown envelope with a South Wales postmark arrives. I tear it open and Richard's smell falls out.

'Beloved Danielle,

'Your letters have really upset me. Our life is granted to us for the duration, but does not belong to us. Our soul is here to fulfill its own purpose. All we can do is work in the right way, moving along our path for its own sake, seeking neither gain, nor reward, nor even comfort. Don't be misled by the "philosophy" of shallow minds.

'You are not alone. Lonely possibly, or dispirited ['dis' from the Latin 'separated from' 'cut asunder' – so, severed from your spirit] and then it is easy to feel alone. But at such times to share a physical experience may prove a diversion, and does nothing to assuage the pain. Real love is a direction, a journey, a searching within; a dialogue with ourselves, independent of the love object.

'If we are "lucky" we are given what we want. But if we are blessed, we are given what we need. And this is not what we are 'needy' for. But rather, we receive as we give, not as we yearn to receive. And whatever you feel you receive from me, know that the gift is not mine, but comes from a higher source.

'I too am feeling lonely, and my soul craves the solace that only your presence can bring. And not only my soul! Dear heart, we shall find a way to be together. But I cannot allow myself to take this step *against* Anna. At the moment constancy is the word, and I make great efforts to keep our relationship sane, balanced and directed for the good of the whole family. My own work, alas, again waits on a back burner...

'Winter has now overtaken us here. Today the wind is desolate, the sea a dull carpet of grey. The animals crouch behind bushes, the small birds have gone into hiding. Dampness will soon have crept into every cranny of the house. And so there is much physical work for me to do: making repairs to the house has become a seasonal occupation! My work now is the maintenance of this home and family, physical and spiritual.

'Dearest one, keep faith. It is the only thing. You are not alone; more than you realize you are not alone. And we shall come again together to those five trees that stand beyond time; they are fragrant.

'My love, as always,
'Richard.'

* * * * * * *

I put Richard's letter under my pillow. But I cannot sleep. His words push up through the feathers, forcing their presence on me like the pea under the seven mattresses of the princess in the fairy story. Stirring the seed inside me. The kick of life; the universe knocking inside my womb. I am suddenly overwhelmed by love for this tiny being struggling inside my body. Thoughts of death are redundant, and I am shamed. Life forces itself upon me from the inside.

And I am driven to dangerous acts of creation. I get out of bed and circle the silent room. I collect the self-pity that I've draped over the furniture, like so much dirty washing waiting for the laundry. I throw off my nightshirt – Richard's shirt, that has embraced my loneliness, that smells of unstopped tears and stale grief. I shall put on a new robe of resilience, worn with cheeky defiance.

I take the notes that I started to write in Wales, three pencils [arranged in height order...] and a rubber, and go back to bed, propping myself up on cushions of collaboration. Fear of the task ahead overwhelms me, then subsides as I let go of the need for perfection. For after all, it is the process that I need to engage with, not the result. The way *is* the goal. The writer's struggle surely lives in the space between language and its interpretation. Words are only the memory of their meaning.

I read through my notes. A fog lifts, in sudden revelation. I discard the notes. I need to write not what I know, but what I need to find: a woman in search of herself, her roots, her ancestors.

'Far far away are my woman roots, planted deep in mother earth. I have lost the memory of her touch on my skin, her smell in my nostrils, her healing in my heart. I have squandered the breath of her wisdom, born in dark places, caressing my dreams. I have forgotten how to stand in the centre of the fire and not burn, how to dance with the spirits in the forest at night, letting their love raise me till I soar. I have forgotten how to reach the source of love and carry it within me...'

Fragments; woman energy, lost belonging.

Beginnings of a story...

Do you hear the wind
At night
Howling
Through the echo
Of my tears…

Sixteen

Depression is setting in with the winter snows. But beyond my window, seasonal frivolity celebrates itself in technicolour splendour. The Spirit of Christmas hovers across the steel and concrete vegetation of the city, and Goodwill Towards Men sparkles menacingly from Oxford Street's decorations. Electric stars glint mischievously in the falling sky. How can I be depressed amongst all this glitter?

The capital streets throng with women on annual pilgrimage to find new fleshpots to show off to their friends; with students buying Good Impressions with charity Christmas cards; with harassed mothers and whining kids queuing up to see the God of Commerce, cheerfully disguised in red hooded suit and long white beard.

At night, groups of small children carol the streets, rattling charity boxes to bribe the faithless to pay for their guilt. And at irregular intervals, the radio screams out its holy admonition: only sixteen, eleven, five, two, shopping days to go! Jesus sits alone in the kitchen and sulks, the Birthday Boy forgotten in the crush.

Some ten million people of all sexes and none live in Greater London. They live in palaces or mansion houses or luxury portered apartments or gracious detached homes or semi-detached houses or condominiums or terraced houses or small flats or poky bedsits or one-night hostels or cardboard boxes. The ostentatiously rich and the invisible poor, bumping into each other with eyes full of curses; pulling down the same sky but seeing different horizons.

London is full of lonely people. And I am one of the lonely ones. I am not old, nor sick, nor really poor; Christmas is no worse for me than other times. But all times are bad. I just want the one I want. And not his marvellous letters of love, nor his promise of a visit 'in the new year', nor his child inside me kicking for her freedom, offer me one gram of compensation. Your distended absence is my only reality.

Richard, Richard… When will you grant my reprieve?

* * * * * * *

And then into my gloom a child's laughter bounces off a family Christmas, a rainbow of colours from a little girl's paint-box, splashed with love. Your eldest daughter's Christmas card arrived today, delayed in the post, out of the blue, into my blue, my blue-black despair. And I howled like a small child given an unbearable treat.

With it a letter from Anna, full of love and concern. And a quote from the Rubaiyat:

"'Neither you nor I know the mysteries of Eternity, / Neither you nor I read this enigma; / You and I only talk this side of the veil…"

'But perhaps we have had glimpses through the veil? Other realities? Everything is possible, no?

'We all miss you. Take care of yourself, and your tummy.
> 'With love,
> > 'Anna.'

How sweet the world is. How nourishing. I am filled with love for Jo, for Anna. But my heart aches with longing for the one, The Only One, who is sitting in the bosom of his family, wrapped in self-preservation, eating left-over Christmas pudding.

I visit the doctor. He says I am 'run down'. [Did you say wounded?] And prescribes twentieth century democratic wonder pills to 'boost my morale'. But not all the laboratories bulging with soporific drugs can numb my loneliness. I bin the drugs and go back to bed.

It is three days after Christmas. When will come the resurrection of love?

* * * * * * *

Beth brings me back from the edge of madness by inventing things for me to do. I am assigned to decorate the flat for her New Year's Eve party. So I spend days playing with crêpe paper and coloured lights and mistletoe, and wrestle with the scrapings of the dying year. And hope that I'm fulfilling her needs.

Everyone seems to be enjoying the party. They play music, and gyrate, and make a loud noise. And people who are my friends bustle around me, offering refreshment, jokes, a body to dance with; forgetfulness. But I am too far away, on the other side of the goldfish bowl; and I haven't learnt to swim.

I've forgotten the rules of the game. Or which game I'm supposed to be playing. So I drink too much and smoke a little pot and get high, and the world no longer seems inimical; just rather oddly funny. When I hear my laughter grating from a long way off, I find myself curled up in Gerry's arms.

He arrived late. He'd been arrested for sitting down at a peaceful demonstration in Trafalgar Square, organized by the Committee of One Hundred, and spent the afternoon locked up in a police cell with other passive resisters. When he was called before the judge, he gave a speech about the terror of the atom bomb, and nuclear disarmament. He was fined six pounds for "disturbing the peace".

Gerry holds my face between his hands, and his look stops my drunken giggles.

'Dani, I've been offered a new job. With The Guardian. I'm really excited. It's a great opportunity. It's – It's in Manchester. I start next month.'

'Gerry, that's wonderful! Congratulations.'

'Come with me, Dani. Marry me. Please. I love you. I've always loved you. I'll adopt your tummy. I'll be all yours.'

I kiss him tenderly, with love, through impotent tears of sorrow.

I go to the bathroom and lock the door and vomit up the party, the drink, the grass. Then I go to bed, cold and sober. And empty.

* * * * * * *

Beth has booked me a hospital bed for The Birth. They sent a form and want to know the date of conception. Hysteria whips my laughter with a horseman's cat-o-nine-tails. The date? It was when the forest was spiked with bluebells and the world was painted gold with my lover's kisses and – But there's no more room on the form.

Another brown envelope arrives from the hospital, menacing with medical meddling. But I am pre-occupied with procrastination, and see no reason to open it. Beth takes charge and nags me, intimidating with facts and figures and sermons against incurring the wrath of the gods in white coats, until it's easier to comply than resist.

All the way to the hospital I keep telling myself that I'm going to have a baby. That's why I must do exercises, and drink milk, and adjust my weight when I walk down stairs. It's why the neighbour's children point and stare, why my parents won't speak to me, why all my dreams are filled with blood. It's why my legs ache, and why my breasts swell, heavy with future significance.

But what has my baby to do with dates, and hospitals, and green vegetables? For smoothed away from all patterns of existence, from the mischievous insinuations of cause and effect, my embryo of love leaps oblivious through the rushing tides of blood, to answer biology with her cries.

I walk through a maze of blue rubber floors, past high windows and doors all leading somewhere else. Someone stops me and says, 'It's not visiting time now,' and I say, 'I'm going to have a baby,' and he says sharp and commanding, 'Wait here!' And then doors open and close and the corridor fills with white coats and mauve and white striped dresses and assorted people inside them and someone says, 'I think she needs the clinic.' And I wonder what I've just been sentenced to.

When I open the door of the clinic, a grotesque mockery of a Kafka novel heaves its weighted welcome. Women of all sizes but one shape writhe on the floor, their huge bellies defying gravity, spindly limbs akimbo. I lie on my appointed mat and think, if only I had a whimsical sense of humour...

The instructress, spitting disapproval, is large and stern as a prison warder and talks as though she personally had invented Human Reproduction. But clearly this has nothing to do with human sexuality, or that act performed on dark nights by wailing alley cats.

Then she brandishes her bulky bosoms to confront me: 'I understand you're not married?'

You understand? You understand that explosion of passion that draws down the stars, that swoons with touch, with nakedness, with night? You four-eyed colossus, wearing your virginity like a prefect's badge over your defensive uniform, you see only tea-cosies of respectability protecting every incubation. You understand? I stare at her. She doesn't have urges, she has Authority!

'No', I say, 'No, I'm not married.' And retreat, into the womb of the Word that was...

* * * * * * *

'I sink roots more deeply into mother earth, plaiting a bond with women far away, warriors who hold up half the sky... Women of all colours, of all languages, known and yet to be invented; languages spoken, signed, drummed; silent languages of touch, of tears, of toil. Women singing over the bones, over the stones that hold the imprint of a thousand dreams. Women celebrating invisible lives, remembering stories that have not yet been lived. Wild women, running with the wind, shadowing our longings, resurrecting our biographies, pouring woman spirit deep under our skin. Women inhabiting the silent places of their souls. Old women, heavy with wisdom, listening to the children. Women's cycles of the moon, dancing with danger. Blood and rebirth...'

* * * * * * *

The days have grown short and the nights intolerably long. Christmas has come and gone, the old year has faded, the new one has been ushered in with worthy resolutions to be recalled with diminishing guilt. Nature performs her own relentless rituals, regardless of human devastation or our pretended role in her accomplishments. For could the prisoner condemned to be shot before dawn be executed, if dawn did not come?

My body grows from one size to another, and the world spins through its pre-ordained orbit, oblivious of the untidy preoccupations of human living. Winter dares to wrap itself up, daffodil shoots pushing cheekily through sodden earth. And still Richard does not come.

He writes to me, beautiful words, words full of love, of promise, of faith in our joined bodies. Our joined future. But they deceive, his words; a continuous instant of bloated hope. Sterile as a palace swollen with eunuchs. Your absence writes things more terrible than you can ever deny.

He writes to me, again: "Show your soul in your face..." Yes, my darling, it shows. It is scarred with longing, with the detritus of passion. My face, furrowed by tears. Don't worry, no other man could want me now. And I have no place to maintain.

You filled my body with your child, and stopped my blood from flowing; but you could not dam up the wildness of my love. What shall I do with it now, my darling? Shall I go out into the night and sing forlornly of my one true love, who lives with another? Here, I shall pick some rosemary for you. That's for remembrance. And here's some rue. But no, no. I'm afraid of drowning.

Would you like some passion? It's a little soiled, but no matter. And swollen. A slight hindrance. But there's plenty left to kindle the loins of all the village boys. And to spare. I can still wrap my thighs round any pair of fresh young buttocks. Just try me.

Dear God, help me. My dreams are all of towers,

spires, poles, witches' broomsticks that I straddle. And round the edges, ghosts of former lust play havoc, delirious with power; then dissolve in lascivious laughter as I wake. My body is one livid bruise of longing.

My loneliness swells with my growing belly. It is more unmanageable. It has no definable end.

* * * * * * *

Soon, I'm going to be a mother. Nature tardily gives a collusive wink and suddenly overwhelms me with instincts that send me rushing to the shops to look at cots and prams and absurdly tiny baby clothes that I can't afford to buy.

Beth says a friend of hers will lend me a cot. Beth says she'll take a week off work to look after us when I come out of hospital. Beth says, it's good to see me finally waking up And she buys two first-size babygros.

My former self rises up to mock me. How can I think of death when birth is the word, rushing towards me in fits and starts and kicks and leaps. I heave my stomach onto the bus in front of me. The conductress smiles as she takes my fare. 'Soon, then?' Soon, yes... Anticipation overtakes fear.

I go back to the flat and start to knit.

* * * * * * *

'Blood and rebirth... Women giving birth, across the world; in fields and huts and rice paddies, beside rivers and streams and puddles, lying on mats or sitting on birthing stools, crouching, squatting, opening their legs as nature receives and blesses her newest children. Women giving birth with women, holding them, soothing them, chanting sacred words, rubbing their bellies with potions and spells; medicine women, wise

women, midwives, crones; the elders of the tribe.
 'Where is my tribe? Where are my elder women?'
 Where is my mother?

* * * * * * *

The pains wake me, sharp and decisive, at two o'clock in the morning. I lie still, trying to contain the fear and the excitement that are chasing each other like wild horses across my stomach. This is the moment, my little one, the moment my whole life has been waiting for.

When my waters break, I wake Beth. She doesn't connect; she thinks of burst pipes, and I burst into tears. I remind her that I'm having a baby. 'At this time of night?' But she hauls herself out of bed and helps me ease my bulk into her car.

Deserted streets echo an eerie silence. I am haunted by a film I saw long ago, or perhaps it's a distant memory? All living matter has been destroyed in the fall-out of an atomic explosion. All that is left is a scrawny scrap of paper, dying in the wind. Is this *the* paper, the one encoded with secret ciphers to ignite a new world?

My pains scream out as ravenous tigers rip at my insides. But my child pins me to my only centre. Past and future lives converge in a blinding flash that lights up the street like a latter-day revelation. I am confident. I glow with a halo of certitude. Oh my baby, be born while my angel of mercy watches over us; and will provide.

The headlights of a lone car speed towards us, flashing across our path two comets of dissuasion, then retreat along our past road, illuminating only our missed opportunities. But we have already moved on, into the dark unknown of the future.

At a deserted junction, Beth obeys the rules of the

road and stops at traffic lights. If they turn green before I've counted to twenty, Richard will be here. Sixteen, seventeen – green! Dear God, let it be true, just this one visitation to buy providence a reason for believing in tomorrow. I've already served my forty days and nights in the wilderness; I've earned my reprieve.

But a drove of flying cranes overhead, or a black cat stalking the night, may mean the contrary. Beth squeezes my hand, a question mark in her eyes. But no, I will not let you wire him to come, not even if you claim sole authorship. I will not go beggar-bowl in hand, with a curtsy of contrition, though not to do so will leave me hollow-eyed with despair. For he knows the time, and the time is now, when angels will dance on the point of a needle, and camels will pass through its eye.

At the gates of the hospital, fear overcomes me. I am punished for looking backwards and stand petrified as Lot's wife. How shall I know what I need to do? I shall cope with the pain, but how shall I manage the mechanics of heaving my bulky expectations into the labour ward?

The white sterile room glares back at me. Menacing shades of the prison house... But my baby shall be born in a warm gentle place, where the air is blossom-sweet and filled with birdsong and the walls are painted gold with sunlight. Why is birth bundled together under one roof with sickness and death?

Hours of pain grind on with terrifying slowness, eroding the bricks of endurance, drip by drip. Drop by drop. When will the hour arrive to crown my baby's head and bring our salvation?

The pain accelerates and I am wheeled into the delivery room, to my baby's first sight of this wondrous world. The air fills with screams evacuated from my bowels; the pain bears down on me, bulls with their tails on fire charging across my mangled body. Richard, Richard... I grip the sides of the bed and try to remember how to breathe, how to push, how to survive the agony. But I am on the wrack, heaving, writhing, moaning, legs strung up, mind and body brutalized with pain and tearing.

And then it's all over, and a voice in a white coat says, 'You have a beautiful little girl.' And I weep. Richard...

They take her away to weigh and measure the exact dimensions of the rewards of love, and I sleep the sleep of the innocent.

When I wake it is already dark, and I sense that I've slept too long. I call out, and the nurse comes running in with such haste, I should have been forewarned. 'Where's my baby?' She shuffles from foot to foot, silent, foreboding...

'Bring me my baby. My baby,' I scream.

The midwife is standing by the bed, wounding me with her calm efficiency as she gives me a cup of tea. 'There's nothing to worry about, dear. Newborn babies often experience a little difficulty in breathing at first. We'll bring her to you very soon.'

She closes the door behind her. Eternity passes, dawdling, before it opens again.

Beth is standing in the doorway, the doctor at her side. I look from one ashen face to the other as they come towards the bed. And everything is written in their eyes that seek so desperately to avert the course of my pain.

'I am so very sorry. But – But she could never have lived a normal life.'

Wailing from the bowels of the earth fills the room.

Beth sits with me and holds my hand until a needle in my arm brings release from a life I could no longer endure.

My darling
Do you not hear me calling
In your sleep?

Seventeen

I can't find the place. It was here before, wasn't it? I've forgotten what it is I'm looking for. There's rue for you, that's for forgetfulness...

I've come back. To find – No, no, that was yesterday. To perform the Last Rites. Where is the priest? He should have been here. It doesn't matter. I'll come back tomorrow.

Do you see the cottage? Yes, this one. With the weeds strangling it by the throat. I could tell you a tale or two about what went on in there. Some goings on, they were. Hot stuff. But I think she was a little soft in the head. It's not important. Who am I? Oh, just a passer-by; of life.

Round the cottage, that's my own private wilderness. Full of dead things. Dead flowers; dead thistles. Dead babies. A moat of memories; defending nothing.

Shall we go inside? No, not there, the window's cracked. Like her sanity, they say. Crushed under boulders of betrayal. Are you hungry? There are the remnants of the last supper stuck to the gas-stove. You can finish it if you like; with Judas. He's already there.

It's better outside. The air outside is fresh. So healthy. Let's sit on the gravestones and weep. This one, this is the one. This grave, here. It's empty. Like my devastated mind.

That's the old oak tree over there. Draped with God's absence.

Are you still there? No? It doesn't matter. Come back next year and water the weeds with your tears. There'll be more of them then. This is a good part of the country for weeds... For tears.

No, no. I can manage, thank you. I don't need help. Just a knife, to carve my epitaph in blood: 'She died of grief in her twenty-first year.' Underneath, an epigram for someone else's life: 'He was her strength; she was his weakness.' But no-one reads the small print, do they?

It's so quiet. Can you hear the silence, humming lamentations? The silence of death, screaming in the dark. Has the world died? No, no, it's just birds in flight, frozen in formation. Blotting out the sky.

Thank you, you may put the coffin down here. Thank you for coming, all of you, all of you. For listening so patiently. It was a dreadful sermon, wasn't it? Goodbye, goodbye. Please leave your dreams in the collection box on your way out. Thank you. We'll plant them tomorrow, by the gravestone...

They've all gone. The living and the dead. No more souls.

Who will bury me? Who will incant eulogies at my tomb?

* * * * * * *

My little one is dead. My child. My sweet precious baby. Ripped from my body. Slow agony of child-birth child-death. Stars shrieking, torn out of the night. The sky full of death. Dead black holes.

My baby: clutching my heart, still beating, in her tiny dead hands.

Ashes to ashes...

"The earth is the Lord's, and the fullness thereof..." Her place is yielded up. So small, so small...

Behind the cottage, soaked with stillborn memories, we bury her.

That's my lover, over there. Weeping grief. The father of my baby. Where were you, Judas, when she pushed through the birth blood, choking for life? Where were you when I screamed your name in my agony?

You came to see her buried. But not to see her born.

But that's all one now. Birth pains. Death pains. I am haemorrhaging grief. It drowns all understanding.

Ashes to ashes...

Far behind come the priest and the rabbi, haggling like fishwives. Whose god? Whose mortal representative? Who cares? No, they are not here. I forgot to post the letters.

They put her in a little box. My baby. I seal it, with the tears I haven't left to cry. We shuffle in silent mourning, the walking wounded tatters of humanity. Shuffling up to that moment that no martyrdom can postpone.

They place her coffin in the earth.

Dust to dust...

I squat on the ground. I shudder with grief. I scratch up handfuls of soil with my nails. I cover it over her. Earth kisses. Dry as dust.

I plunge. The gaping wound of earth receives me. I lay my body across my baby's coffin. My breasts weep warm milk, splattering the earth crimson.

My baby has drowned in the bloody deluge. Who will bless her immortal soul? The fishwives...

No prayers; that would be a blasphemy. And no obsequies. Only eyes bleeding immutable grief.

By the grave, my lover stands with me. He holds my hand. He brushes tears from his eyes.

There are no words between us. There are no words left. Death has murdered words.

* * * * * * *

The weeds grow tall over the graves of the innocent. That's my baby down there. My child. The rewards of love. Hush, she's asleep now; don't wake her... I would you could.

Somewhere, on a lavatory wall, God scrawled "Nietzsche is dead!" We are both dead, but no-one has noticed.

Why don't you bury me? Here, this is the grave. No, it's not too small.

Can any creed provide a single text to salvage even a touch of hope from this wreckage?

"Time was created that suffering might end." Scholars and men of divinity jump in, where angels might have feared... "Suffering is the school of the soul; endurance the best teacher."

My eyes whip them with hysteria. They glint in the dark, a mad woman's legacy. They see nothing but devastation.

My baby is dead.

* * * * * * *

All night long you rock me in your arms.

In the morning, you say, 'Where shall I take you?'

And I say, 'Take me home.' Only, I don't know where home is.

You take me back to Beth's flat. You stay with me for a week. The seven days of ritual mourning. We sit on low stools and friends bring food and kindness.

When I won't eat, you feed me, spoon by spoon, like a baby...

On the eighth day, you rise. You kiss my forehead, and you say, 'I have to go back to Wales. For a while.'

And I say, 'Yes.'

And you say, 'I'll write to you. Dearest heart.'

And I say, 'Yes.'

But my baby is dead.

* * * * * * *

There is nothing left. Not love, nor pity, nor grief. Nor even despair.

I am far far beyond that island of life that once embraced human experience. Love, remorse, joy, sorrow, they're all one now, all thrown onto the same dung-heap of human debris. Suffering and happiness are equally meaningless, equally remote. The worms that will eat my rotting flesh will not differentiate.

I asked so little of this world: not a nice house, nor fashionable clothes, nor fame, nor popularity, nor notoriety, nor money in the bank, nor poise, nor beauty, nor acclamation; nor even wisdom. I could have learnt to live without books and music and the comfort of friends; sunlight, birdsong, the smell of fresh cut hay.

I asked only the love of the one that I loved the one chosen one out of all the billions of ones that crawl the surface of this earth. Just the one that I wanted. And the life of our child. Everything that I have in life or would ever have in the future to be bargained for the one that I want, and our child. It was a simple message, God. How did you get it so scrambled?

Well, you can go away now, God. There's nothing more to take. Except my life. Except my life, which I gladly surrender. But that, it seems, in your infinite sadism, you refuse to take. I am condemned to live. To wander. Forty years in this wilderness of perdition.

"The reward of sin is death." But only, it seems, for those who wish to live.

God, if you return from your vacation, answer me this: why do you accept the prayers of the corrupt, and not the bargains of the innocent?

Well, I've said all the prayers that I've ever learnt. And some that I hadn't. It's all over now. My baby is dead. My lover has gone. There was only ever love and death. Now there is no more love.

* * * * * * *

Nothing claims me any more. No one can buy me, for I have nothing left to lose. And long ago I relinquished my passport to the human race, my sanity.

I am quite calm now. "Tragedy is restful..." All hope and doubts are vanquished. I shall do what I have to do.

So, Socrates, Jesus, Joan, move over in your hallowed graves. Make room for another crucified fool! It's all in vain. I know. All martyrs die in vain. Even those who die to save the world from itself. Especially those who die to save the world from itself.

When I was little, God lived in heaven. When I grew up, God died, and I resurrected him in my heart. When I am dead, what will happen to God?

Well, I can't worry about that now. Anyway, you died without caring what would happen to me.

So, this is it. Pull down the blinds, another prodigal daughter is making her final bow!

The world has turned to water. Rivers wink at me as they rush past in the deluge. But there is only one that claims me, one that waits, knowing...

The cottage dissolves in my tears, the wilderness with its blooms of death tumbles into the flood. My cradle of love is rocked by the hurricane, roaring lullabies as it dashes it to pieces on the cliffs.

The world is floodlit by my brilliant desperation. I am running, blinded by time, towards that one river, that draws me like a magnet. It is my siren of doom. It pulls me, spellbound, to my own destruction.

A long way off, an old oak tree crunches its branches in the wind; a weeping willow hangs her head in sorrow. But the river rushes on, seduces me with subaqueous smiles, makes a loud noise. My place is yielded up...

Oh, the water is so cold. It is rising around me. I am all flooded over. The dove can find no resting place for the sole of her foot.

Tomorrow winks collusion, resurrection pouring from its third eye. But I am past all watery wooing; future persuasion has died a muddy death.

My lover stands over me, gazing down, weeping streams of solace over my effigy. The letters of his name float above the cataclysm, sodden with aborted beginnings.

Now my lover is holding an olive leaf between his lips. I strain upwards. He opens his mouth to kiss me, and the olive leaf floats away on the river of his grief. But his streaming kiss sails down to me, through bubbles of love. Down through the weight of all the oceans, his kiss reaches me; the seed of love, planted in the grave of the sea.

See, I have prepared myself for you, my love, pure and fresh as summer rain, with a shroud as my bridal dress, and a wreath of amorous fishes swimming through my hair. Round my throat, a necklace of river weeds tangles with death...

Come, lie with me, my darling, and spread our wedding sheets over this watery womb. It is sterile as the cold juice of love that sticks across the withered cave of my sex.

Oh I am drowning... Don't weep, my love, don't weep, there was no other way. Give me your lips, just one more time... My beloved is mine... Your kisses make waterfalls of my blood...

A fountain of gardens, a well of living waters... Oh I am drowning. But is it water, or blood. I can't quite see...

There. Now you can gather me in your arms, as you gathered me for love so many worlds ago. I am frozen, white. Only my breast is streaked red, where I carved your name.

Now everything is still. The water has closed over me. There are no more ripples to show where too much grief was drowned.

What legends of love shall be washed up on the riverbank with my body?

Now, everything is still. Silent.

Silence, holding the universe.

Perhaps that is the only religion; how we interpret the silence around us.

My darling, my love, how do you interpret the new silence around you?

Oh Richard, Rich —

Epilogue

But it didn't happen that way. The sun has been shining all day, and no-one commits suicide while bathed in sunlight.

So I sit by the river, watching eternity wash through the waves at my feet... Once, in another life, someone I loved wrote to me: 'We cannot know what we are without first dying that most harrowing of all living deaths...'

To reach what breaks in us. Then we can rise. We arrive at who we are by accrual.

To have contemplated death seriously grants a refreshing perspective on life. Recognition that we are each an infinitesimal speck in the vastness of the cosmos; and that simultaneously we hold within us all the riches of the universe. That the human heart can hold profound paradoxes that the head cannot grasp. And that only in the contemplation of death may we come to understand time, and our need to create it.

To have contemplated death also grants a refreshing perspective on love. What we call 'love': an expression of our need. 'What we want is not what we desire, but what we lack...' So we 'choose' someone to save us from ourselves. We are all looking for salvation.

I sit at the edge of the world watching the river... Random thoughts fragment the air: the way I have courted tragedy, which creates dramas of its own; giving substance and context to our lives. Camouflaging fear. And fear, of course, lies behind what we call 'love'. It is fear that drives us to jealousy; to want security, ownership, promises. To be safe.

So we construct our own limitations. We create them for ourselves, or we allow others to create them for us. And then we suffer. But there is no value in suffering. *'To suffer is to allow...'* It is our choice whether we suffer or not. And suffering is ultimately an acute form of self-importance.

Slowly, I am waking up. The task is to lay bare the raiment of gold beneath the covering sackcloth of mourning. We are all blind, tapping with our white canes, but we know the path is there.

Suddenly, a flicker of truth. But truth is not sudden; it is always there. What may be sudden is our perception of it; the evolved instant at the end of a long road. Truth may find us out in small hidden corners, washing the floor, or cleaning the toilets. It doesn't have to come in dramatic ways, or in idyllic surroundings. Truth will find us when we are ready to be found.

The world gives me a nudge. I need to interpret the wounds of my life; not to evade my destiny, but rather to fulfill it in its true potential – the imagination. For I see now that what most wounded me as a woman, may most nourish me as an artist. Only then can I truly let go. And so set myself free. The real teacher, I realize, is not endurance, but release.

My shadow on the grass remembers other things: moments that are two moments: the occurrence and the memory of it. Looking back in order to give meaning to memory. To arrive at that place where unbearable truth is preferable to comfortable fiction. Perhaps this is the writer's journey, to travel between the lines of experience and its memory; to inhabit that murky space in the cracks between, that time misses.

If pain is the breaking of the shell that cocoons wisdom, then art is the only metamorphosis that justifies the struggle. The struggle to get beyond the ego, to lose oneself in order to create the art. Another paradox, of course, because in the very act of creation, we are most truly ourselves.

A moment of grace, caught in mid flight; seeking to invoke the ultimate healing silence of art. The awakening of spirit, that grapples with the limitations of the medium itself. To reach beyond form, beyond the symbols of paint or musical notes or words, to that sacred space where the work itself may be set free to dream. To reach a recognition of a universe in love with itself.

Perhaps I am writing now in order to save myself. And one day, in the far future, I may reach that magical place where I shall write because I am saved.

Anyway, it is my only means of competing with God. Of recognizing God within me. Which is reason enough.

In the Beginning was the Word...

** These lines were taken from poems written by Anthony Hayter.